A Murder of Crows

Terry Nolan
Copyright 2021

Printed by Kindle Direct Publishing

This is a work of fiction. Names, characters, organizations, places, events and incidents are either products of the author's imagination or are used fictitiously. Any resemblance to actual person, living or dead, or actual events is purely coincidental.

Cover design and illustrations by Ghislain Viau
Creative Publishing Book Design

ISBN 978-1-7348533-2-2
e-book 978-1-7348533-3-9

Dedication

Warren, Shelly, Josh and Zac

My sister, Faye and Dan, her husband

ACKNOWLEDGEMENTS

Thanks to my editor Staci Mauney with Prestige Prose

Thanks to Ghislain Vaiu with Creative Publishing Book Design for the book cover and sketches.

Thanks to Mary Wagoner, a friend, a neighbor and most importantly a retired teacher. She assisted in proofreading the manuscript one more time before submission to the publisher.

Thanks to Patti at Patti's Hallmark in Edmond, Oklahoma for allowing me to sell my books in her store.

Other Books by Terry Nolan

Forbidden Forest

A Murder of Crows

Table of Contents

Chapter 1	First Day	1
Chapter 2	The Bully	10
Chapter 3	Happy Birthday Willow	20
Chapter 4	A New Teacher	27
Chapter 5	A Strange Encounter	33
Chapter 6	Science Class	38
Chapter 7	A Visit to Mr. Hardy's House	44
Chapter 8	Crows	51
Chapter 9	Underwood Family Nursery And Tree Service	56
Chapter 10	The Library	63
Chapter 11	Sequoia	69
Chapter 12	Trouble	76
Chapter 13	Into the Woods	83
Chapter 14	A Change of Mind	88
Chapter 15	Dad	93
Chapter 16	Uninvited	99
Chapter 17	Pooka	105
Chapter 18	The Journey Begins	111

Chapter 19	Take Cover	117
Chapter 20	Witch Island	125
Chapter 21	Ultimatum	136

Chapter 1

First Day

Elm raced up the driveway on the first day of school as the driver turned the school bus around and blew the horn. It wasn't a good sign to miss the bus on the first day. *Oak Valley Middle School* was painted on both sides of the bus along with a drawing of a live oak tree. This late August day was going to be hot and humid.

The kids on the bus lowered the windows and yelled, "Run Elm, run." One called out, "Run Forrest, run." Everyone laughed as they closed the bus windows. Elm's dog, Sequoia, barked from the end of the driveway. Elm wondered if the dog was barking, "Run Elm, run."

The driver kept the door open. Elm leaped onto the first step, grabbing hold of the handrail to steady himself before continuing up the next two steps. He looked down the aisle for his best friend and neighbor, Randy.

"The next time you're late, I'm going to leave you." Mr. Loomis laughed. His skinny legs were so long, he had the bus seat pushed back as far as it would go, and his legs still looked cramped.

"Sorry," Elm said. He knew Mr. Loomis wouldn't leave him. Spotting his friend, he hurried down the aisle. Out of breath, he slumped into the open seat next to Randy and placed his backpack on the floor between his legs. He wiped sweat from his forehead.

"Really, can't you ever be on time?" Willow murmured as she spun around in her seat and stared at her brother. Her red curls bounced around her shoulders.

"Mind your own business." Elm scowled. He took off his baseball cap and dragged his hand through his brown hair. "Sisters." He rolled his eyes.

Elm owned dozens of caps, but the one he had on today was new. It looked just like the old ones except it wasn't dirty. A white hat with the black letter H for Hawks—the school's mascot.

Randy arched an eyebrow. "Do you plan on being late every day? Maybe I should call you to make sure you're on time."

Elm punched him in the arm. "Don't be a smart aleck. I forgot something and had to run back to my room. Then I grabbed a piece of toast from the kitchen, and now—here I am."

The bus made another stop along the way, picking up three more kids. It would take about fifteen minutes for the bus to arrive at the school. Riding along the two-lane county road, something in Elm's peripheral vision caused him to shift in his seat and glance out the window.

A Murder of Crows

"Randy, look." Flying beside the bus—no, not by the bus, but only next to the window where Elm and Randy sat—flew about fifty crows. "Did I tell you that a flock of crows is called a murder of crows?"

"Yes. That's weird. But after what happened a few weeks ago, I can understand why they're called that." Randy shuddered. He had been attacked by giant crows not long ago in the forbidden forest, and Elm knew Randy would never forget it.

Elm observed the crows keeping pace with the bus. Their beady right eye seemed focus their attention on him, while their left eye kept them from flying into each other. The other children on the bus whispered and pointed at the window. A half-mile from the school, the birds flew upward and disappeared. Elm squinted into the sunny sky, but the crows were gone. "Don't you think that was strange? I wonder—"

"It's just a coincidence," Randy said.

The bus pulled into the long, curved drive and stopped in front of the middle school. Elm and Randy stayed in their seats and stared out the window at their new school.

Elm took a deep breath and let it out slowly. "It's not fair!"

"I agree," Randy said. "What a waste of half a day."

"Okay, boys, get off the bus," the driver yelled.

They grabbed their backpacks and clambered down the steps onto the oversized cement walkway leading up to the front doors. The sidewalk was partly shaded by the rows of live oak trees lining both sides of the walkway. Elm glanced skyward, but not seeing any crows or any other type of birds, he joined Randy to gawk at the sprawling two-story building. Elm had lived in Oak Valley his whole life and had been around the school many times. Oak Valley Middle School was twice as big as the elementary school. From the main entrance, two wings spread out to each side.

"Hey ladies, what're you waiting for—an invitation?"

Elm turned to see Kobe strolling up behind them. He and Elm had shared the same classroom and teachers since first grade.

"Let's get moving," Kobe said. "We're finally in middle school, and I can't wait to meet some of the seventh- and eighth-grade girls."

"You really think they'll give you, a sixth-grader, a second look?" Elm snickered.

"With my good looks and the cologne, I'm wearing, they'll be after me in no time." Kobe took a small comb out of his pocket and drew it through his raven-colored hair.

"You're one of a kind. Besides meeting all the girls, answer me one question. Why do they make us attend half a day before Labor Day weekend? It doesn't make sense, and it's a waste of time." Elm moaned. "Why can't we meet our teachers next Tuesday? How hard can it be to find our classes?"

"Stop whining, Underwood." Kobe enjoyed calling people by their last name. He glanced at the boy standing next to Elm.

"This is Randy. Randy, this is Kobe." Elm introduced his friends.

A Murder of Crows

Kobe slapped Randy on the back. "Welcome to the neighborhood."

"Thanks, I think," Randy said.

They walked toward the entrance. Even though there were several sets of doors they could use to enter the building, they were jostled around by other students as everyone tried to squeeze through the same set of doors. Girls' high-pitched voices called to their friends, and boys high-fived or fist bumped with friends they hadn't seen since May.

The principal stood next to his office doorway which was the first door on the right after entering the school. He towered over the students and most of the staff. In a baritone voice, he repeated, "Slow down! No running! Sixth-grade classes are on the first floor. Check your maps."

The three boys moved out of the flow of students and stood against the wall.

"Which way?" Randy asked while orienting his map to their location.

"Our homeroom is 130," Elm said.

"Follow me," Kobe said.

After a short distance, students spread out in all directions. Seventh and eighth graders sprinted up a wide staircase to the second floor. Behind the steps, lockers lined the wall. Four corridors led in different directions. The one closest to the stairs had a sign with an arrow pointing toward the cafeteria. Another sign indicated the science rooms and labs were down the farthest corridor. Straight ahead and out the back door, a covered walkway led to the gym that doubled as an auditorium.

Elm pointed. "These two hallways have room numbers."

"This way," Kobe yelled as he turned the corner.

Together they walked past more lockers and several classrooms. Doors banged open and closed as students scurried into their homerooms.

"Here we are." Kobe opened the door and held it for Elm and Randy.

The smell of fresh paint assaulted Elm's nostrils. Bright beams of sunlight streamed through windows that looked out toward the lush green grass. Glancing around the room, Elm saw the desks were set up five rows across with aisles between them and six desks per row. Most of the brainy students selected the desks closest to the front of the room. The kids that always seemed to be in trouble sat at the back. Elm found three desks side by side in the middle of the classroom and close to the windows.

Several students called out to Elm and Kobe. They knew everyone since they had all attended elementary school together.

"Whoa, who's that with Elm?" A girl raised her eyebrows. Lucinda was the only girl in the room with purple streaks running through her long blonde hair.

The bell rang as the last of the stragglers rushed into the classroom.

Mrs. Cleary stood at the front of the room. She'd taught middle school for five years. "Everyone, quiet down and take your seats. Check your schedules and your maps. When the bell rings, you'll be on your way to your first-period class.

A Murder of Crows

Since this is only a half day, you'll spend approximately fifteen minutes in each class, then you'll return to this room before you go home."

Elm, Randy, and Kobe had already figured out all their classes were together.

"This year is going to be great," Kobe said enthusiastically.

When the bell rang, students rushed into the hallway. Elm waited for some of the kids from the back of the classroom to pass by before he stepped into the aisle.

As Elm approached the front of the room, Mrs. Cleary stopped him. "You can't wear that cap in school. Put it in your locker before you go to your next class."

Elm took a deep breath then replied, "But it's the middle school mascot. Go Hawks!" He usually wore a baseball cap everywhere he went. He had an uncanny feeling that someday a hawk would rescue him if he were ever in trouble, though no hawk had helped him in the forbidden forest.

"Sorry, it's not allowed in school," Mrs. Cleary said sympathetically.

She waited. Elm removed his cap, folded it up, and stuck it in his back pocket. He looked past her into the hallway and saw Randy and Kobe waiting for him just outside the door.

"In trouble already," Kobe snickered.

He shrugged. "Not funny. Let's go before we're late."

Time flew by as they moved from one classroom to another. When they walked into the last class of the day, a man with a mop of shaggy hair, thick glasses, and a paunch stood in front of the whiteboard.

"Is everyone ready for school?" Mr. Hardy, the science teacher, asked.

Most of the students replied yes, and a few moaned.

"We'll be studying earth science...astronomy. Are you interested in the stars and comets?"

"We already studied the planets," Elm said.

"This is totally different. It's not just the study of the planets and where they're located. It's the study of the sun, moon, stars, planets, and other non-earthly bodies and phenomena. I've scheduled several nights throughout the year to meet after dark. We'll use a telescope and observe the amazing activities that can't be seen with the naked eye. I think you'll find it very interesting."

"Will we see spaceships or aliens?" a student asked.

"I don't think so, but you can never be sure what's out there."

"If we have a telescope, may we bring it to the outing?" another student asked.

"That would be great." The bell rang. "I'll see everyone on Tuesday." As the students left the room, Mr. Hardy gathered up papers and slid them into his briefcase.

Walking back to homeroom, Elm said. "I think this is going to be a very interesting year. I may even enjoy school."

Mrs. Cleary welcomed the students back to homeroom. "I hope everyone found their classes without any problems. As most of you know, I had a baby girl during summer vacation." The girls clapped and cheered. She continued, "I'm only here today. As of next week, you'll have a new homeroom teacher.

She's coming from another school district and wasn't able to be here today."

The hairs on the back of Elm's neck tingled, and a knot tightened in his stomach. It was the same feeling he'd had when he entered the forest.

The bell rang.

"Have a wonderful Labor Day weekend," she yelled as the students rushed out of the classroom.

Elm hoisted his backpack up, grabbed his cap from his pocket, and put it on. He looked around. Nothing seemed out of place, but he still had a knot in his stomach.

Chapter 2

The Bully

A figure lurked in the distance and watched the students hurry out of the building and jump on their bus. Spotting Elm, a wicked smile curled her lips upward. A large crow flew down and landed on her shoulder.

*****

As the first bus pulled away from the curb, Randy said, "Hurry up, or are you planning on being late for the bus again?"

"Ha, ha, funny. Let's go." Elm had the feeling someone was watching him, but he glanced around and only saw other students.

Grabbing a seat in front of Willow and Juanita, Elm and Randy sat side by side. Elm turned toward his sister. "We didn't see you today."

A Murder of Crows

"All my classes are on the second floor except science—it's on the first," Willow said. "All science and computer labs are located there. Randy, what did you think of the school?"

"Most of the students and teachers seemed friendly and no one treated me like the new kid."

"That's good. I think you'll like it here."

Twenty minutes later, they arrived at home. Sequoia greeted them with a ball in his mouth and his tail wagging. Willow took the ball and threw it toward the house.

"Hey, I'll see you tomorrow, and I won't be late for the bus on Tuesday," Elm said.

"See you." Randy rushed across the lawn to his house.

"Willow, wait." Elm stopped walking. He searched the area but didn't see anyone around except his sister.

"What?" She looked at him suspiciously.

"Mrs. Cleary said a new teacher will be here next Tuesday."

"So?"

"So, when she said it…well, when she said it, I got a bad feeling," Elm said. "The sort of feeling something is going to happen."

"No, Elm. I don't want to hear it. No otherworldly adventures, no magic. My birthday is this weekend. It's all I want to think about." Willow turned and walked away.

Sequoia rubbed against Elm's leg and whined.

"I know boy. Something just doesn't feel right. Maybe if we go to the treehouse, the trees will reveal some secrets to us."

It wasn't actually a house in the trees—more like a platform with rails around it. Elm climbed a ten-foot homemade ladder that was nailed to the tree. Mr. Underwood had built it several years ago, but not without the trees' permission.

Recently, Elm and Willow found out they could hear the trees talk. It was an odd inherited trait from their father's side.

Elm sat down and waited. A light breeze ruffled his hair, and he strained his ears for even a whisper. The trees were silent.

So far this month, the trees had been eerily quiet. Hopefully, that was a good thing, except Elm remembered Willow said the other day the trees said something to her. What had they said?

*****

On the first day of Labor Day weekend, Elm watched as his mom pulled two hot pans out of the oven and set them on the counter. She was in the middle of making Willow's birthday cake.

"It really smells good in here," Randy said as he licked his lips.

"Sorry, no cake until tomorrow," she said.

"Mom, we need to go to town," Elm said. "We'll take our bikes, okay?"

"Why?" she asked.

A Murder of Crows

"We"—he pointed at Randy— "still need to buy Willow's birthday gift."

Mrs. Underwood leaned against the counter. "Elm, you're always putting everything off to the last minute. Don't buy any junk. Willow's a teenager now. Try to find something nice that she'll like."

"Yeah, Mom," he muttered as he and Randy left through the kitchen door. They rounded the corner of the house to pick up their bikes and leave.

Ten minutes later, they rode past the Welcome to Oak Valley sign. Three more miles and they turned onto Main Street and rode by the town square then the library. The library was a huge three-story Victorian home with a turret on one side. The house had been remodeled fifteen years ago into a library. Rumors said the house was haunted.

Oak Valley was a small town, but it had a movie theater, a bowling alley, and a skating rink for entertainment.

They pedaled through the parking lot of the big box store on the far side of town. After placing their bikes in the rack in front of the store, they strolled inside. They each had fifteen dollars. The first stop was the electronics department—not to look for a gift, but to browse the cell phone section.

"I can't wait until my parents buy me a phone." Elm searched through the glass at phone cases, looking for one that might have the school mascot on it.

"Yeah, I think I might get one for Christmas," Randy said. "At least that's what I'm going to ask for. What are we gonna get Willow? I don't think she wants toys. Maybe jewelry?"

"Too expensive." Elm looked around searching for the girls' department. "Let's check out the clothes." One last glance at the cell phones then Elm headed to the girls' area of the store.

As they walked around, they looked at blouses, then sweaters.

"This feels weird being here," Randy said.

"I hope no one sees us—uh oh, duck." Elm grabbed Randy's shirt and jerked him down behind the counter. He placed his finger to his lips. "Shh." They peeked over the edge. "See that boy? That's Kyle. He's a bully."

"I can't believe we're hiding in the girls' department. If someone spots us now, they're really going to think we've lost our marbles." Randy pointed to his head and drew a circle.

Kyle wasn't much bigger than either of them, but he seemed to strut instead of walk. They watched him for a few seconds. A young mom passed Kyle. Her son lagged behind her. As the little boy neared Kyle, the bully threw up his arms in front of the kid walking like a zombie and grunting. The boy bolted and grabbed his mom's hand. The lady glanced back. Kyle smiled. The lady smiled back. Again, when the woman wasn't looking Kyle took a step and raised his hand as if he would hit the boy. The kid screamed. Kyle disappeared down the shoe aisle before the lady could turn around.

Elm and Randy stood up, and Randy huffed. "I can't believe he scared that little kid. He needs to pick on someone his own size."

"Oh, believe me, he does. If he sees us, he'll tell everyone in school we were hanging out in the girls' department." Kyle had bullied Elm throughout elementary school.

"It's Willow's birthday," Randy whispered. "We're just buying her a gift."

"Kyle lies. He'll tell everyone we were going through the girls' underwear. Let's hurry, find something, and get out of here. Hey, look at this." Elm held up a T-shirt with a picture of a girl riding a bike. "It's only five dollars. I think she'd like this."

Randy nodded approval and picked up a bundle of socks. "Check these out." He threw them at Elm.

"These are great. She'll love'em." A unicorn was on one pair, a girl riding a bike on another, and a third one had a young witch holding a wand. "And they're only six dollars. We'll have enough money left to go to the movies on Monday."

"What's playing?" Randy asked.

"The new Marvel movie."

"Sounds like a plan," Randy said.

Glancing around and not seeing Kyle, they hurried to the checkout line, paid for their items, and left the store. Waiting outside next to their bikes sat Sequoia.

"Hey, buddy when did you get here?" Elm said to the dog. "Let's go to the park."

They rode into the park located across from the town square. They stopped near the basketball courts to see if anyone they knew was playing. After dropping their bikes on the lawn along with their purchases, they saw a group of eight and nine-year-old boys running away from the court.

Elm gazed through the fence. "Oh no. How did they get here so fast?"

Kyle and two of his cronies, Roscoe and Brody, were laughing and bouncing a basketball.

Focused on making hoops, the boys were unaware of Elm and Randy's arrival.

One of the younger boys ran out of the fenced area around the basketball court toward Elm. "He stole my basketball," the boy cried.

"Don't worry." Elm turned and walked through the gate onto the court with Randy beside him. Sequoia growled but lay down in the shade next to their bikes.

"Well, looky, looky, if it's not the flower boy and his shadow." Kyle elbowed Brody. His friends chuckled at his comment. He always called Elm the flower boy because Elm's father was an arborist and his family owned the Underwood Family Nursery and Tree Service. Kyle threw the basketball with all his strength, hitting Randy in the stomach. Randy doubled over the basketball as the air left him with a *whoosh*.

Elm kept his eyes on Kyle. *What have I gotten myself into?* His thoughts were interrupted by the child talking to someone.

"They stole my ball."

"What's going on here?" Mr. Hardy stopped next to the young kid. "You three, pick up the ball, and give it back to him."

A Murder of Crows

Kyle clenched his fists and his friends didn't move.

"Kyle, I have your parents on speed dial. Do you want me to call them?" Mr. Hardy pulled his phone out of his pocket.

Kyle didn' pick up the ball but instead snapped his fingers. "Let's go." As he passed Elm, he collided with him, knocking his cap off, and whispered, "I'll see you later, flower boy."

Mr. Hardy watched as Kyle and his buddies left the area, then said, "Are you guys, okay?"

They both nodded. Elm picked up his cap and the basketball. He handed the ball to the boy.

"Thanks," the kid said. Bouncing the ball, he returned to the basketball court.

"Are you Mr. Underwood's son?" Mr. Hardy asked.

"Yes, and my sister, Willow, was in your class last year," Elm said.

"She's a very smart young lady," he said.

Elm laughed.

He looked at Randy. "I saw you in my class on Friday, but you don't look familiar. Are you new around here?"

"Yes, um, yes, sir," Randy said. "I moved here just over a month ago. I live next door to Elm."

"I'm sure Elm's family has already warned you, but I'll mention it. Don't go into the forest behind Elm's house."

"I've been told, and no, I don't plan to go into the woods." Randy winked at Elm.

Just past Elm and Willow's backyard was an area called the forbidden forest. People who ventured into the woods seemed to get lost and were sometimes never seen again. When Randy and his family moved next door to Elm, the two boys and

Willow immediately became best friends. During the first week of August, they ventured into the forest. What happened to them next would stay a secret between them. They would never go into the woods again.

"See you in class on Tuesday." The science teacher turned and walked away.

The sun slid behind several dark clouds. Elm turned and started toward the bikes. "Looks like it might rain any minute. Let's go home. I don't want us or Willow's gifts to get wet." A chill flowed through Elm. He squinted toward a group of trees but didn't see anyone.

*****

Again, in the distance next to a tree stood an old hag. Above her, on a limb sat a black crow. The old hag watched as they pedaled away. Soon…

When Elm escaped through a portal last month, the old hag had tried to follow him into this world, but the portal closed before she could crawl through it. Anger stirred inside her because it had taken her a month to find a new portal, and she blamed it on Elm.

Now she was able to go back and forth through the portal from her world to this one. She was here to stock up on juicy morsels to feed her enormous carnivorous plants, and maybe in the process she would drag Elm away to her world and keep him there.

A Murder of Crows

Chapter 3

Happy Birthday Willow

The scent of sweet butter and maple syrup drifted up the staircase. Every Sunday morning, they had waffles and bacon for breakfast. On his way to the kitchen, Elm stopped and banged on Willow's door. "Happy birthday! It's time to eat."

Willow opened her door. "All you ever think about is food." She followed him down the steps and when she entered the kitchen…

"Happy birthday, Willow!" their parents said in unison.

"I'm making your favorite breakfast." Mrs. Underwood said as she placed a bowl filled with scrambled eggs on the table. She removed the sizzling bacon from the pan and onto a dish. Stacked high on another plate were chocolate chip waffles. Elm's stomach rumbled as he sat down at the table and held his fork and knife in his hand. Sequoia lay under the table waiting for any scraps that fell his way.

"It's the same breakfast you make every Sunday," Willow said.

A Murder of Crows

"Honey, it's special today—your waffles have birthday candles." Mrs. Underwood stuck thirteen candles into a stack of three waffles.

Elm jiggled his feet under the table waiting. Willow wiped sleep from her eyes as she sat down. Wrapped gifts surrounded her plate.

There was a knock on the back door, and Randy walked in carrying another gift. "Happy birthday, Willow." He laid the present on the counter and eyed the plates piled high with waffles.

"Randy, would you like to join us for breakfast?" Mrs. Underwood asked.

"Hmm are you going to open your gifts first or eat?" Randy looked at Willow.

"Eat, so it doesn't get cold," Elm said.

"Guess I'll have waffles," Randy said. "With bacon, please."

When everyone finished eating, Mr. Underwood helped his wife clean off the table. She wiped up a few sticky areas where syrup had dripped.

"Honey, time to open your gifts." Mrs. Underwood smiled.

Willow tore off the paper on her first present. "I love it." She held up the T-shirt Elm had bought. Next, she opened the gift from Randy. She laughed. "These are great." She showed the socks to her parents. "Look, there's a pair with a girl on a bike. It matches the T-shirt. I'm going to wear these tomorrow to the movies."

Mr. Underwood handed her a gift. "This is from your mom and me." The box was not small but not quite as big as a shoebox.

Willow's eyes glistened. "I know what it is."

"Do you?" Mrs. Underwood asked.

Willow ripped the paper off the box revealing a cell phone. She jumped up and hugged her mom and dad.

"Thank you! Thank you! Thank you!" She squealed. "I love you." She held the phone in her hand. "Can I call my friends?"

Mr. Underwood nodded.

"Wow," Elm said. "Will I get one on my birthday?" Elm's twelfth birthday would be October twenty-ninth.

"Are you going to be thirteen?" Mr. Underwood asked.

"No."

"There's your answer," he replied.

"Dad." Elm groaned. "That's not fair."

"We can still use your walkie-talkies to talk to each other," Randy said.

"Yes, not as good as a phone, but it will do for now. I'll give you one when we come back this afternoon to keep at your house. Willow, do you want to go to town with Randy and me?"

She held up a finger for him to wait a minute. She was already talking to Juanita. When she hung up, she said, "Why are you going?"

"Since it's your birthday, we're going to the ice cream shop."

"No. I'm going to the Tea House later for my party."

The Tea House was a unique place. It had two areas inside—one area for anyone to order food and have tea, and the other section was reserved for special events. Young girls and ladies wore fancy hats with feathers that were provided by the tea house. They sat at tables where they were served tea and crumpets. No, not crumpets, but little cakes like petit fours. It was a girlie party for Willow and friends.

*****

The weekend passed quickly, as weekends do once school starts.

"I'm glad we have an extra day before going back to school," Elm said as his mom drove him, Willow, and Randy to the movie theater. The three of them sat in the back seat of the car together.

"Look at this." Willow showed Elm and Randy all the whistles and bells on her new cell phone. "I've already downloaded several games."

"Willow, don't be playing with your phone while you're in the movie." Mom stopped in front of the theater.

"I hope I don't have to wait until I'm thirteen to get a phone," Elm whined while climbing out of the car.

"Maybe you'll get one for Christmas," Randy said.

They entered the theater and the smell of freshly buttered popcorn drew their attention to the concession stand. Several of their school friends stood in line buying refreshments.

"If we don't hurry up, we're not going to find seats together," Elm said.

"I'll find the seats," Willow said. "You and Randy buy the stuff. Don't forget to get a large box of Whoppers so we can share it."

The theater had twelve different movies on the marquee, but it seemed everyone was headed to the Marvel movie. Elm and Randy entered the theater with their arms full of goodies. The lights had not dimmed yet, and they spotted Willow saving two seats close to the front of the theater. Previews of coming attractions were showing on the screen. All around them people whispered and laughed. Way in the back of a theater, a small child could be heard asking questions and the parents shushing him. The lights darkened, the voices lowered to a hum, and the movie began. Elm, enthralled by the action on the screen, leaned forward. He forgot about everything else—even eating his popcorn.

Once the movie was over, and they stood outside, Elm said. "Oh my gosh, that was great. I could watch it again."

"Me too," Randy agreed. "What did you think, Willow?"

"Any movie with Scarlett Johansson in it, is good. She's a real kick butt, take no names female." Willow laughed. "Now, let's go to the ice cream shop. I need to tell you what I saw yesterday."

"We spent all our money," Elm said.

"I got birthday money. I'll buy you a milkshake."

"You are the best sister."

A Murder of Crows

"I'm your only sister, loser. I called Mom earlier to let her know we'd be at the ice cream shop after the movie."

They turned away from the theater and walked down the block. Inside the shop, Elm ordered the same thing he got every time—a chocolate milkshake. Randy had a blueberry shake, and Willow asked for vanilla.

Willow took a few sips of her drink, then glanced around. She whispered, "While I was at the Tea House yesterday afternoon, I saw something very strange. Mr. Hardy went into the library with a woman."

"What's unusual about that?" Elm asked. "We saw him yesterday too, but he was alone."

"Something was off...for one, the library was closed. And two, it wasn't his wife or the librarian."

"How do you know it wasn't his wife?" Elm raised his eyebrows.

"The woman was tall and thin, taller than Mr. Hardy, and his wife is not thin. The woman had a black hoodie on and she held it tight around her face as if to make sure she wasn't seen on any cameras."

"Maybe he got the key to the library so he could do research for his class," Randy said. "He told us we'd be studying astronomy."

"Hmm, maybe you're right," Willow replied. "But I don't think they give the key out to just anyone. And who was the woman, and why was she hiding her face?"

Elm ran his fingers through his hair—something he did when he was nervous or concerned.

"When I left the tea room before I got into the car," Willow said, "the leaves on the nearby trees shook. Then I heard—or I thought I heard—'Don't trust her.'"

"Who is her?" Randy asked.

"I don't know. And not sure I want to."

"I went to the treehouse yesterday afternoon hoping the trees would reveal information," Elm said, "but they were quiet."

"All I can say is Mr. Hardy, a female stranger, and the library after hours is definitely not normal," Willow said.

Chapter 4

A New Teacher

The next morning Elm was early to the bus stop beating Randy to the end of the driveway. Randy wasn't far behind him. With everyone on the bus in a timely manner, the driver arrived at school before expected. Walking toward the building, Elm passed other students standing around chatting about what to expect for the first full day of classes. As he neared the entrance, the wind picked up, and a shiver ran down his spine. The trees along the school's walkway rustled and a muffled voice said, "Beware!"

He spun around to see who was behind him. Spotting Randy, he said. "Did you say something?"

"No. What did you hear?" Randy knew Elm and Willow's secret about hearing trees talk, and he glanced up at the branches.

"Never mind. It's just my imagination working overtime," Elm laughed even though a sense of dread tumbled in his stomach.

When Elm entered the classroom, the whole room was rearranged. Instead of five rows across there were now seven rows with very narrow aisles between them. Each row had two desks added to them—almost double the student capacity. Biting his bottom lip, he absentmindedly pulled his cap from his back pocket and put it on his head.

"What's going on?" Randy asked.

Lost in thought, Elm didn't answer right away. "I don't know but let's get seats next to the windows before they're all taken." He hurried halfway down an aisle, squeezed between the desks and chairs and sat at a desk next to the window. He then laid a book on the two adjoining desks for Randy and Kobe.

"Hey, you better take that cap off before you get in trouble," Randy said.

"Huh?" Elm reached up and touched the cap. He removed it and stuck it back in his pocket. Hearing a familiar voice, he spun around and saw Willow, along with Juanita, walk into the classroom. Behind them more seventh graders crowded through the door.

"What are they doing here?" Elm asked. He watched as the seventh graders pushed sixth graders out of their seats and told them to scram to the other side of the room.

Willow set her backpack down at a table with her friends, then walked over to Elm. Before he could say a word, Willow said, "The principal told us our classroom was vandalized over the weekend and we had to report here. He wouldn't even let us look in—he just stood there blocking the doorway. Now we're stuck with sixth graders." Willow glanced at Juanita. "This can't be happening. I can't be in the same homeroom with my brother."

A student near the door yelled, "Shh, I hear the teacher coming."

Several older students threw wads of paper at him and laughed. A low buzz filled the classroom as chairs scraped against the floor and students quickly found their seats. Click, click, click. The sound of high heels clacking against the hallway's tile floors echoed into the room. The closer she was the louder the click, click, click. Everyone's eyes were glued to the door.

A hush fell over the room as the new teacher entered. The boys gasped as their eyes widened and their jaws dropped. The girls held their cell phones below the desk texting each other. Elm smiled at first, but then goose bumps popped up on his arms. The teacher, a gorgeous young woman with coal-black hair that hung down to the middle of her back, stood at the front of the classroom. Her flawless skin was accented by her ruby red lips. She wore skin-tight black leggings covered by an emerald-green tunic. Her high heels were five-inch stilettos that looked like sharp blades attached to her the bottom of her shoes. With every step she took, her heels clicked against the tile floor.

"Good morning," she said. "I'm Ms. Agnes Crow."

Elm shuddered then bumped Randy and pointed toward the window. Outside sat ten to fifteen crows. Their black eyes followed Ms. Crow's movements as if waiting for a signal. Suddenly, Ms. Crow raised her hand above her head for no apparent reason. The birds outside took flight and disappeared.

"Girls put your phones away unless you want me to take them and give you detention this afternoon," Ms. Crow said. "The reason this group is sharing a class is—"

The door banged open and Kyle strutted into the room.

"You're late," Ms. Crow said.

Kyle stopped and turned to her. "Whoa, you're a babe." He smirked. His buddies burst into laughter but stopped abruptly when Ms. Crow glared at them.

She walked up to Kyle, her nose only inches from his. "You will stay after class when the bell rings."

"Gladly." Kyle took a step back and eyed the teacher from head to toe. Instead of walking to the back of the room to sit with his friends, he stood over a girl in the front row. "Scram," he growled. The kid almost burst into tears. She grabbed her books and scurried to another desk.

Ignoring Kyle, Ms. Crow continued, "I'm your homeroom and science teacher. A few changes to your schedules have been made. Mr. Hardy suddenly had to leave town. I'll be combining sixth- and seventh-grade classes since you'll be studying the same information. The class will be held after lunch. I don't want the first period when everyone is still sleepy, nor the last class of the day when everyone is tired and not listening to what I have to say." She smiled, but Elm noticed the smile didn't show in her eyes.

The seventh graders groaned. Elm glanced at Willow.

"But today you will have study hall instead of science. I still need to bring several items from home to the science lab."

"Where did Mr. Hardy go?" Willow asked.

"What a strange question to ask me." Ms. Crow said with bitterness in her voice. "How would I know—I don't know the man. I was informed this morning that I would be teaching his science class."

"Didn't I see you with him Saturday evening going to the library?" Willow insisted.

Some of the students held their breath. Others whispered to each other. Ms. Crow glanced around the classroom. She inhaled deeply as if trying to control her voice, then continued talking.

A boy sitting near Elm leaned across the aisle and whispered, "If all middle school teachers look like her, sixth grade is going to be the best."

"Do you have something to share with the class?" Ms. Crow suddenly appeared next to the boy's desk without a sound. Ice cold blue eyes stared down at him. The boy's face turned as red as a radish. Then he grinned up at her and slowly shook his head. "I recommend you don't speak until you are asked. Do you understand?"

The boy nervously nodded his head. He resembled a fly caught in a spider's web.

Turning, she leaned over, placing her hands flat on the desk, her face almost touching Elm's. "Do you have something to say, Mr. Underwood?"

"No." Elm cringed. *How does she know my name?*

As quietly as she arrived at his desk, she was back at the front of the room. No clicking. Elm glanced at her feet. She wasn't barefooted—she still was wearing her sharp, bladed stilettos. How did she walk without making any noise?

"I don't know how your other teachers treated you, but that's the past. I'm interested in every one of you. Besides having you in homeroom and science, I'll monitor your progress in other courses."

Elm didn't hear anything she said. His mind was reliving last month's terror. Willow, Randy, and he had encountered giant crows after being pulled underground by a huge live oak tree. Could these be the same crows, but regular size? Hadn't he seen an old hag during his escape? He couldn't remember. Then there was the magic—

The bell rang and the students stood up to leave.

"Did I say you could leave?" Ms. Crow slammed her hand down on her desk. Everyone sunk down into their seats. Tension filled the air. "You will not leave until I excuse you." She took a deep breath. "You may now exit the room."

Elm grabbed his books and headed for the door. He couldn't get out of there and away from Ms. Crow fast enough. Only Kyle remained at his desk, a silly grin on his face.

Chapter 5

A Strange Encounter

"What a witch," a female student said as she passed Elm and Randy in the hallway.

"Who cares how strict she is?" Kobe said as he caught up with Elm. "She's beautiful, and I couldn't take my eyes off her."

Is she a witch? Elm wondered. His first year in middle school—he hoped there wasn't going to be a problem...a supernatural problem. *She's just a new teacher, and a little bit mean. That doesn't prove she's—*

Willow tugged on Elm's backpack. He spun around his heart racing. "Don't sneak up on me. You almost gave me a heart attack."

"I didn't sneak up on you. You were deep in thought and not paying attention to your surroundings." She pulled him over to the wall and out of the way of the students rushing to class. "I came to tell you...something's wrong. That's the same woman I saw with Mr. Hardy."

"What?" Elm asked.

"The other night when I was at the Tea House—" The first warning bell rang through the speaker above their heads. "Oh, I have to go I'll talk to you later." Willow vanished up the staircase.

Elm caught up to where Randy waited in the hall for him. "What was that all about?" Randy asked.

They had only thirty seconds before the late bell rang. Hurrying toward their class, Elm said, "She thinks Ms. Crow is the woman she saw with Mr. Hardy the other night at the library."

"Whoa, Mr. Hardy and a good-looking teacher." Randy snickered.

They entered the English classroom just in the nick of time. Elm watched the clock. The morning classes dragged. He couldn't concentrate because each time the teachers began their instruction, the door opened and Ms. Crow entered. She nodded to the instructor and slipped to the back of the room. The teachers acted surprised to see her, but they all acknowledged her and returned to teaching their subject. Elm sensed her gaze on the back of his head, but he stared straight ahead, determined not to turn around. He felt a great uneasiness about Ms. Crow. *Who is she? Why does she seem so focused on me? Is it just my imagination?*

*****

A Murder of Crows

After lunch, Willow met up with her friends on the second floor. The girls gathered in the restroom on the way to science class. The restroom had been remodeled since last year. The walls were a bright white and the stall doors had inspirational messages painted on them, such as *Work Hard, Dream Big* and *Bloom* with flowers painted around the words. There were other messages. Some of the girls laughed at it, but Willow thought it was inspiring.

"Can you believe it—we're finally in seventh grade, and we're stuck in a class with sixth graders," Juanita said. "Why couldn't we at least have been with the eighth graders?"

"I agree," Maggie said. "You know, my boyfriend is in eighth grade, and we would have had a good excuse to be together every day for studying."

"Well, most of our classes are on the second floor," Lou Ann said. "Just think of all the handsome older boys we can meet. Talking about cute, your neighbor has gorgeous blue eyes. I could just melt when he looked at me."

"His name's Randy." Willow said. "He moved here from the city. Not much of a country boy. He and Elm have become really good friends."

"Sure." Juanita snickered. "And he's good friends with you too."

Changing the subject, Willow asked, "Don't you think it's strange that Mr. Hardy just up and left?"

Lou Ann shrugged her shoulders. "Who cares?"

Willow glanced into the mirror to admired herself as she combed her hair. Today she wore a new royal-blue T-shirt and jean shorts. Her favorite colors for clothes were royal-blue and kelly-green—they both made her red hair redder and her green eyes greener.

The door squeaked open. Willow watched as Ms. Crow entered the room. The overhead fluorescent lights flickered and dimmed. As Willow's eyes adjusted to the shadows, she gaped at the mirror. She wanted to look away but was mesmerized by what she saw. It wasn't the reflection of Ms. Crow but an old hag that stood in front of the mirror. The hag was bent over, unable to stand straight. She had stringy hair and snaggled teeth that showed through a creepy smile. She in no way looked harmless. She stretched out her arms, reaching for Willow.

Stumbling backward, Willow snatched her arm out of reach and knocked her books off the counter. Her friends jumped as the books crashed to the floor. She sucked in her breath, then exhaled, and closed her eyes for a second.

"You okay?" Juanita asked.

"You look a little pale," Ms. Crow said, "as if you've seen a ghost."

"I'm fine. Just a little dizzy, but I'm much better now." Willow kneeled to pick up her books. She watched her friends' reactions, but the other girls only glanced at her, then formed back into a circle in front of one of the stalls, whispering. Shivering as she stood up, she looked back at the mirror only to see the reflection of herself and the teacher.

Ms. Crow pointed at the words painted over the mirror, *Mirror, mirror on the wall, there's a leader in us all.* "I don't think that applies to you, Willow," she whispered.

A Murder of Crows

Willow stared at her, shocked.

"Don't be late for class, girls," Ms. Crow said in a pleasant voice as she walked out of the room.

Willow swallowed a lump in her throat. "Did you hear what she said to me?"

Juanita looked at her baffled. "What?"

"It was totally creepy," Willow said. "First, I swear I saw an old hag. How could she be in the mirror and not in this room? Then Ms. Crow told me I would never amount to anything."

"You're kidding, right?" Juanita asked. "You're losing it, girl. You've been acting strange since your birthday party at the Tea House."

Before Willow could reply, the warning bell rang. Everyone except Willow rushed out of the restroom headed to their next class. She pushed open all the stall doors. She was alone—no one, no hag, just her. It had to be Ms. Crow.

Leaving the restroom, she jogged down the hall and reached the science room just as Ms. Crow closed the door. Willow grabbed the doorknob.

"A second later, Ms. Underwood, and you would be spending detention with me this afternoon." Ms. Crow sneered.

The hairs on the back of Willow's neck stood up.

Chapter 6

Science Class

Elm and Randy entered the science class. The room had been rearranged since Friday when Mr. Hardy stood at the teacher's desk. Last week the walls were painted a dark blue and black. The solar system hung from the ceiling, and the walls had posters filled with stars, their names, and their location in the sky. On one of the walls hung a giant poster showing a closeup of the moon's surface. The room made Elm feel like he was in space, but now the solar system and posters were gone. The walls were a bright white and along the window ledge sat flower pots filled with plants Elm recognized from his dad's nursery. A row of narrow tables lined the wall behind the teacher's desk. On them live grasshoppers, beetles, worms, and butterflies jumped, crawled, and flew around, trying to find an escape from the mason jars that kept them prisoner.

Elm bit his lip to make sure he wasn't having a nightmare. *Why would a teacher want to teach sixth graders about the darkness of carnivorous plants?*

The students' desks resembled the configuration of the homeroom. The seventh graders grabbed the seats on the left side of the room next to the windows, leaving the sixth graders to sit on the right. Elm took a seat next to Randy and behind Kobe.

"The first half of this year, we'll study my favorite subject—Eaten Alive." Ms. Crow pointed toward the potted plants. "These are carnivorous plants. They eat bugs and small mammals. There are over six hundred species. We'll study only a few of them. They can usually be found in marshes, swamps, peat bogs, or muddy areas. They are so ingenious in how they trick and lure insects into their traps. Depending on which type of plant it is, it will either snap its leaves together crushing its prey, or drown it. Some of the plants have different techniques to capture their food. The sundews have tiny sticky hairs that capture insects. And then there is the bladderwort that sucks the bugs into their tubes."

Everyone sat still and watched as she opened a jar and pulled out a large grasshopper. Elm knew what was coming next. Since they had just eaten lunch, he was sure someone would throw up.

"I know all of you have heard of the Venus flytrap." She dropped the bug between the leaves of the plant. Suddenly, it snapped shut, and Elm heard the crunch of the bug being smashed. The students nearest the front gasped.

She pulled a butterfly out of another jar with tweezers. "This is a sundew." She placed the insect on the sticky hairs. The beautiful butterfly flapped its wings trying to escape, but it was stuck. The plant curled its limbs around the butterfly, and the bug stopped struggling.

"That's fascinating," a seventh grader said.

She laughed. "I plan to allow each of you to feed the plants. Who's interested? I'll make a list."

Eager to be on the list everyone raised their hands except Elm, Willow, and Randy.

"Ugh, no thanks," Willow said.

"I'm surprised at your reaction, Willow. Doesn't your father have carnivorous plants at his nursery?"

"Yes, but I don't feed them," she said.

"No time like the present to learn more about these plants." Ms. Crow eyed Willow like a bird eyeing a worm. "Some people will be on the list more than once. There are plenty of books about these plants in the town library. I expect you'll be spending a lot of time there."

"Why can't we use our computers at home?" a student asked.

"I prefer you use the library. I'll see you there. Correct?" She looked around the room as everyone nodded.

A boy raised his hand, and Elm along with the other students turned around in their seats.

"Yes?" Ms. Crow smiled. "Malcolm, you have a question?"

"You said the plants can eat small mammals," Malcolm said. "I just wondered how. Those plants are so tiny."

"These plants are small because they're in pots," Ms. Crow said. "In the wild, they grow much larger. I've visited an area where some of these plants were as big as small trees."

"Wow. Where?" another student asked.

A Murder of Crows

"All in good time. You'll learn more about them, and you may even see the larger plants before this school year is over." Ms. Crow raised her eyebrows and smiled.

One of Kyle's buddies, Roscoe, yelled out, "I haven't seen Kyle since homeroom. Did one of those giant plants eat him?" He chuckled.

"No," Ms. Crow replied. "But if you don't start raising your hand to be called on, you may be the first one the plant eats."

Malcolm's hand flew up, but he didn't wait to be called on. "Good one, Ms. Crow. No one will miss Kyle or his buddies because they're bullies."

The bell rang. No one moved. "You may leave," she said.

Everyone rushed out. Elm came out of the classroom just in time to see Roscoe barreling toward Malcolm. Elm didn't want to see Malcolm get hurt. He squeezed through students that were blocking his way. He stopped just as Roscoe bumped into Malcolm knocking his books out of his hands. Other students walking nearby backed away.

"You better watch your mouth, or you may be the one that disappears," Roscoe said.

"Sorry, Roscoe. It was only a joke," Malcolm squatted to pick up his books.

Roscoe pushed him over with his foot. "Well, I'm not kidding. The next time the teacher isn't around, I'll stick your face into one of those pitcher plants and see if it will suck your brains out." Roscoe turned and walked down the hall.

Malcolm laughed and turned to Elm. "He doesn't get it. Pitcher plants don't suck the insects into them."

"Be careful, Malcolm," Elm said. "You don't want the bullies targeting you."

As the hallway came alive with students rushing to their next class, several students commented, "Carnivorous plants sound a lot more interesting than astronomy."

Elm spotted Willow and hurried to catch up with her, but before he could speak, she said, "I have to tell you what happened in the girls' restroom."

"Ew, not sure I want to know," Elm said.

Willow punched him lightly on his arm. "Don't be a jerk. What I have to tell you has to do with Ms. Crow."

The clicking of heels against the tile grew louder and closer.

"I'll talk to you later." Willow sprinted up the staircase to her next class.

Elm had the feeling that something unusual was about to occur. He headed to his next class, but his mind wasn't on learning. *What's happened to Mr. Hardy? Where's Kyle? Where did Ms. Crow come from?*

When the last bell of the day rang, Elm and Randy met up with Willow before leaving the building.

"I wonder what happened to Kyle," Elm said. "He didn't attend any classes today."

A voice behind them said, "I wouldn't worry. He went home sick." They turned around and found Ms. Crow standing inches from them with a sneer on her face.

A Murder of Crows

They rushed out the door and jumped on the bus. On the ride home, Willow told them about the reflection in the mirror.

"I don't believe Mr. Hardy moved away," Elm said. "I want to go to his house after we get home. Randy, do you want to go with us?"

Randy didn't answer immediately. Then he slowly nodded his head. "Sure, I'll go, but I'm hungry."

"Great!" Elm said. "We'll take time for a snack, then tell our parents we need to go to the library, and we'll go to Mr. Hardy's instead."

Chapter 7

A Visit to Mr. Hardy's House

The school bus pulled into the driveway, turned around, and let Elm, Willow, and Randy off. Sequoia waited for them with a ball in his mouth. Elm automatically took the ball and threw it. Tongue hanging out, Sequoia darted after the ball.

"Remember the other day?" Willow asked. Sequoia skidded to a stop beside her and sat down, his ears pointing upward in a listening mode. "I told you the trees said not to trust her, but we didn't know who 'her' was. I think it's Ms. Crow."

"I think you're right," Elm said. "Did you see the birds at the window when she told us her name?"

"No."

"They were crows," Randy said as he walked toward his house.

Willow glanced at Elm. He called after Randy, "We'll see you in thirty minutes." He then told Willow how the birds flew into the air when Ms. Crow raised her arms.

A Murder of Crows

Sequoia retrieved the ball and dropped it at Elm's feet.

"Not now, boy, we have things to do." Elm went to his room and typed the name "Agnes Crow" into the computer search engine. Lots of names popped up with Agnes and others with Crow, but there was not a single Agnes Crow. Strange. He checked Facebook and Twitter—still no Agnes Crow. Either she wasn't into computers, or she didn't exist.

Forty minutes later, they headed out the door as Mr. Underwood came home from work. "Whoa, where are you going in such a hurry?"

"To the library," Elm said. "We have research to do."

"You can't do it on the computer?"

"Dad!" Willow said. "We have a new teacher, and she gave us an assignment that we can only find in books at the library."

"Uh-huh," Dad muttered as he checked the clock on the wall. "Be back before it gets dark."

Elm and Willow rushed out of the house. Randy waited at the end of the driveway on his bike. As they pedaled away, Sequoia trailed behind them. When they were a mile from the Welcome to Oak Valley sign, Randy took off pedaling as fast as he could go. The race was on. Every trip to town, they raced on their bikes to the sign. Usually, Elm came in first, then Willow, and Randy last. This time Randy was determined to be first. Suddenly a large crow flew across the street in front of him. He skidded to a stop.

Elm laughed as he rode past Randy. Willow was close behind. When they reached the sign, they waited for Randy.

"Hey, that wasn't fair," Randy grumbled. "Did you see that crow almost fly into me? And you two didn't even stop to see if I was hurt."

"All's fair in a race," Elm said.

"Are you okay?" Willow giggled.

"Some friends you are," Randy said. "Yes, I'm okay. That bird deliberately tried to fly into me."

As they continued on their way, Elm glanced into the blue sky. A few light clouds flowed across the sun making shadows on the ground. There weren't any crows around—actually, no birds at all soared across the blue yonder. Riding close together, Elm told them about his search on the computer and not finding any information on Agnes Crow.

"What do you think that means?" Willow asked.

"Not sure," Elm replied.

They rode past the front of the library and turned left onto Magnolia Road. Behind the library was the town's cemetery.

"I didn't know the cemetery was here," Randy said. "No wonder everyone thinks the library is haunted."

"It's not haunted," Willow said.

Elm slowed down and glanced through the wrought iron fence surrounding the cemetery. Stopping, he said, "Hey, I have a great idea."

"You think all your ideas are great." Willow giggled as she placed one foot on the ground and looked through the fence.

Elm ignored her. "Next month is Halloween."

"So?" Willow said.

A Murder of Crows

"So," Elm said, "what if we get permission to plan a scavenger hunt in the cemetery?"

"That sounds creepy," Randy said. "Let's do it."

"Deal." Elm pushed off on his bike still glancing through the fence. A breeze swept through the leaves of the trees near the graveyard. *No ghost, but something's wrong.* Elm listened, but the trees weren't talking. They crossed First Street.

"Isn't this the street your grandfather lives on?" Randy said.

"Yes," Elm said. "Several blocks that way." He pointed. "Mr. Hardy lives on Fifth Street, we're almost there."

Slowing down, they came to a halt in front of Mr. Hardy's house, chill bumps covered Elm's arms.

"I guess Ms. Crow was right," Willow said as she stared at the yard.

The grass needed cutting. It was waist high. The flower beds were all dead—but if Mr. Hardy was out of town, well that made sense. They walked onto the porch. It was covered in leaves and dust. They rang the doorbell. No one answered.

"Ring the bell again," Elm urged.

Someone inside pulled a curtain back and peeked out the window.

"Look," Randy pointed.

A click sounded as the lock was released. A woman in her early forties opened the door and stood just inside. She wore black jeans and a flannel shirt. The buttons on the shirt were misaligned with the buttonholes. Her brown hair stood up all over her head. It looked like she had forgotten to comb it. Her eyes were glazed over.

"Can I help you?" Mrs. Hardy said with a slur.

Elm stuttered. "Isss Mr. Hardy hom...home?"

"Are you his students?"

"Yes," Willow blurted. "Yes, we're his students, and we need to talk to him about our assignment."

"Come in."

They stood just outside the door. Elm glanced at the other two, waiting for one of them to take the first step.

"Can he come to the door?" Randy asked.

"Hurry, come in. He just arrived home and he's very tired. You can talk to him in the living room."

Elm stepped across the threshold. The smell of cooked cabbage assaulted his nose. He liked cabbage, but at the moment his stomach lurched. The others followed. Inside the house, dim lights threw shadows against the walls. Mrs. Hardy shuffled across the floor, hardly lifting her feet. She pointed towards a huge, comfortable recliner.

"There he is. Please don't stay long. He needs his rest." She turned and ambled toward the kitchen.

The three stood gazing at the recliner in amazement.

"Holy crap, is she on drugs?" Randy whispered.

Mr. Hardy's jacket was spread across the back of a chair with each sleeve resting on the arms. His pants hung down from the seat with his hat on his lap. A pair of shoes sat on the floor in front of the chair. But there was no Mr. Hardy.

Elm shivered. "This is too creepy for me. Let's get out of here."

A Murder of Crows

They rushed out the door and heard Sequoia growling with his hackles up. Caw—five crows sat on the rail around the porch. They turned their beady eyes from the dog to the children. Caw—caw, it sounded as if they were laughing. They flapped their wings and flew away.

"She's watching us," Willow cried. "I'm afraid. Who is she? What is she?"

Elm couldn't help noticing an old woman across the street standing bent over. She wore a shabby jacket with a hood and held a cane in her left hand. Long, stringy salt-and-pepper colored hair hung down and shielded her face, but he knew she was watching them.

Randy followed Elm's gaze. "Is that a witch?"

Willow jerked around. "Oh my gosh, that's the woman I saw in the mirror."

"It's just an old lady. Let's go," Elm replied, unsure of his answer.

They hopped on their bikes and rode away. Sequoia continued to bark as he followed them. In the distance, they heard the cackling of a woman—or was it a witch?

Chapter 8

Crows

The following day, Elm, along with all the other students watched Kyle lurch up the sidewalk. His hair stood straight up, like porcupine quills. Instead of strutting with his head held high, he slouched past his buddies bumping into Brody.

"Hey, amigo," Roscoe said. "What happened to you yesterday? How was detention with the new teacher?" He snickered.

"Watch it!" Brody pushed Kyle knocking him to the ground.

All the students gasped and backed away. They waited for Kyle to jump up and pounce on his best friend. Kyle stayed on the ground for a moment, then slowly lumbered to his feet, tilted his head to the right, and continued to amble into the school. At a distance, everyone followed whispering.

"What happened to him?" Randy asked.

"Does he remind you of someone?" Elm said.

"Huh? Who are you talking about?" Randy replied.

"Mrs. Hardy," Willow said "Remember how she stumbled through her house? She slid her feet across the floor and almost tripped several times before she made it to the kitchen."

"Oh yeah, and she thought her husband was sitting in the chair," Randy said. "That was weird." They followed Kyle into the school. Kyle bumped into the door, then reached for the doorknob, opened the door, and tripped across the entrance. He didn't fall but stopped at the first desk. The students who usually sat in the front row jumped out of their seats and dashed away from him.

Homeroom went completely silent—no whispering, no laughing, nothing. Ms. Crow stood behind her desk as she glanced at everyone, her eyes landing on Kyle, and she smiled.

"What did you do to our friend?" Roscoe broke the silence.

"I didn't do anything." Ms. Crow's smile disappeared, and her lip curled up into a look of disdain.

"Then what's wrong with him?" Brody snarled. "He was fine until he stayed after class with you."

Ms. Crow let out a high-pitched laugh. "You two—would you like to stay behind in my classroom while the others go to their first-period class?"

Their mouths fell open as they stared at her. "No! No way!" They both replied in unison.

Everyone giggled nervously. They'd never seen the bullies afraid of anyone before.

A Murder of Crows

Turning back to the rest of the class, Ms. Crow said, "I'm in a very good mood today. You may go ahead and leave before the bell rings. I'll see everyone in the science lab after lunch." She dismissed the class.

Kyle didn't budge as Elm walked past him.

"What do you think happened to Kyle?" Willow asked.

"Did you see his eyes?" Elm asked. "They were glazed over like Mrs. Hardy's. I think Ms. Crow did something to both of them."

"Let's talk later," Randy said. "We're going to be late if we don't hurry."

"See you." Willow hurried up the staircase to her next class.

Elm's first three periods went smoothly. It was now time for lunch. Unlike the sterile, uninviting elementary cafeteria, where everyone sat at long tables with stools attached, this room had about twenty-five round tables with either four or six chairs. The ceiling curved with an arch and had recessed lights. On one wall hung a large bulletin board covered with information from school clubs. The food service was located along another wall, and behind it was the kitchen. You could watch the staff preparing the food. Windows stretched across another wall facing the parking lot.

As they stood in the serving line, Randy said, "Wow, look at these choices. I'm going to sample some of everything."

"It's definitely not elementary," Elm said. "In elementary, you knew every Monday was meatloaf and every Thursday was pizza and there were no other choices. We're moving up in life. I wonder what they serve in high school?"

Terry Nolan

After going through the line, they found a table near a window. The room which was usually filled with the noise of students talking and laughing, now had everyone talking quietly.

Randy listened for a second. "Everyone is whispering about Kyle and how strange he acted. Don't you wonder why he didn't show up for any of our classes?"

"Your hearing seems to get sharper every day," Elm said. "Before long, no one will be able to keep a secret from you." He laughed.

"You're just jealous because you can't hear them," Randy said, then he wolfed down his lunch. "This is one of the best school lunches I've had this week." Randy scraped his chair back and stood up. He carried his tray to the dirty-tray area.

The cawing of crows vibrated in Elm's ears. The skin on the back of his neck prickled and his stomach muscles tightened. He approached the windows. "Check it out."

Crows hovered above the parking lot.

"That's a lot of blackbirds," Kobe said.

"Not blackbirds—they're crows," Randy said.

They watched as the birds swooped down then flew upward toward the sky in a formation of blackness. They swarmed in a circle then began another dive.

"Oh crap! Ms. Crow is in the parking lot," Kobe yelled. "They're going to attack her. I can't watch." He ducked down below the window.

Randy turned his back to the glass.

A Murder of Crows

"They're not attacking her. She's controlling them." Elm stood spellbound watching her raise her arms in the air. Her lips moved as she chanted words he couldn't hear. More crows joined the group. They flew straight up, turned in a circle, then flew directly toward the window. Elm took a couple of steps back and squeezed his eyes shut so tightly his brows furrowed.

One, two, three he counted before opening his eyes. The birds disappeared. Elm's heart pounded against his chest. He glanced around the cafeteria to see the other students' reactions, but no one else was aware of what was happening outside. They were enjoying their lunch, studying, or playing around. No one saw the crows.

"They're gone," Elm said.

"Did they hurt Ms. Crow?" Kobe asked.

"I told you, she was controlling them," Elm replied.

"What's wrong with you?" Kobe stared at Elm. "How can she control birds? You've been complaining about Ms. Crow since yesterday. Get over it. She's great." He stomped out of the room.

"Kobe!" Randy called then looked at Elm. "I believe you. Do you think—"

"She's from the underground." Elm finished his sentence. He nodded. "We need to talk to Willow."

Chapter 9

Underwood Family Nursery and Tree Service

Ms. Crow entered the Underwood Nursery. She was surprised by how busy the store was in the middle of the week. Even though Oak Valley was a small town, people from all over the county and even the state shopped here.

The nursery was more than just plants and trees. It was a mercantile store. Built in an old red stable that had been cleaned up and remodeled many years ago, it was divided into several sections. One area sold produce, canned jams and jellies from local farmers, and candies you don't usually find at a grocery store. Another area sold seasonal merchandise. As of today, it was filled with pumpkin candles, ceramic turkeys and all things Halloween or Thanksgiving. The greenhouse was filled with shrubs, perennials and mums for the fall.

A Murder of Crows

*****

Mr. Underwood stood in the greenhouse checking his supply of chrysanthemums to see if he needed to order more before the end of September. He turned when he heard the bells over the door tinkling. He watched as a beautiful lady walked toward him. The overhead fans blew wisps of her hair slightly as she tilted her head giving the effect of the women you see on television in shampoo commercials. Mr. Underwood was mesmerized.

"Hello, Mr. Underwood. I'm Ms. Crow, Elm and Willow's science teacher." Her voice was smooth like silk.

He cut his eyes away, then looked back at her. "Is there something wrong?"

She let out a light giggle that seemed to surround him like music. "I see where Elm get his brown hair and beautiful eyes. I'm sure he'll be as handsome as you when he's older."

Stunned by this personal observation, Mr. Underwood asked again, "Is there something wrong? Are the kids in trouble?"

"Do your kids usually get in trouble? No nothing's wrong. I'm teaching the class about carnivorous plants and Elm mentioned that you had several species. I thought I would stop by and check them out."

"I would be happy to personally show you what we have." Mr. Underwood smiled and took her arm in his as they walked toward the back of the greenhouse. This was not something he did with other customers.

"I've never heard of a science teacher teaching about carnivorous plants," Mr. Underwood said. "It should be very interesting for the students."

"Oh yes, it's my favorite subject. I already have a few plants, but I understand you have some gorgeous sundew plants. I would like to add them to my collection."

"I have three different types. I'm sure you already know there are over a hundred species of sundew."

"Yes." Ms. Crow pursed her lips.

Mr. Underwood took a step closer to her and said in a soft voice, "I have the smallest sundew, called the dwarf, also a few medium sizes, and two of the *Drosera magnifica.*" He glanced around and took a step back. His reactions to her were out of control.

"That's amazing," Ms. Crow said. "I would like to buy both of the *Drosera magnifica.*"

"You are aware this plant can grow as large as a bush," Mr. Underwood said.

"Yes." Ms. Crow seemed to quiver with excitement.

Mr. Underwood opened a door, and they entered a temperature-controlled room filled with tropical plants. He then pointed out the two plants she was interested in. They weren't very big, but it wouldn't take her long to grow them to their full height.

She relaxed and smiled up at him. "There are my babies. I can't wait to take them home."

He watched as she seemed to float across the floor to the plants. He shook his head, trying to shake off the feeling that he was in a trance. Being around Ms. Crow was a little unnerving.

"We have special soil for the plants, if you're interested," Mr. Underwood said.

"Thank you, but I have everything I need already at home." She picked up the plants, turned around, and headed for the door.

Outside of the tropical room, she stopped. "There is one more thing I need to talk to you about."

"Yes?" He took a few steps away from her so he could think straight.

"I like for my students to study at the library so they can use the reference section and work together as a group. I noticed that neither Elm nor Willow have bothered to visit the library."

"They haven't?" Mr. Underwood remembered Elm telling him on several occasion they were going to the library. "We live a little outside of town. Don't you think using the internet would be just as easy rather than finding information in reference books?"

Her blue eyes turned dark. "I want my students in the library, you do understand?"

"I'll talk to them this evening. Thanks for stopping by and I hope you enjoy your new plants." Mr. Underwood quickly stepped away from her. He went into his office and closed the door. He then called his father on the phone.

"Hey, Dad, how are you? Has Elm or Willow been by to see you lately?"

"No, I haven't seen them since school started. Is something wrong?"

"I just met their new science teacher, and, well, um, she seemed very strange," Mr. Underwood said.

"She? I thought Mr. Hardy was their science teacher."

"Seems like he quit or left town. Not sure what happened to him. The new teacher is named Ms. Crow. Maybe it's just my imagination, but she definitely seemed odd."

"The kids haven't been by or contacted me about anything weird going on. I'll let you know if I hear anything."

"Thanks, Dad," he said.

Hours later when Mr. Underwood arrived at home, the scent of fried chicken filled the air. Following the savory smell into the kitchen, he noticed chocolate cake on the counter.

"Dinner's ready," Mrs. Underwood said. She had prepared his favorite meal—fried chicken, mashed potatoes, green beans, and chocolate cake.

He wondered if she knew he had made a fool of himself at the nursery. "Is something special happening tonight?"

"No, I was just in the mood to fix chicken," she said. "Did everything go well at work today?"

"Umm, mentioning work." He glanced at Elm. "Your teacher stopped by the store."

"Which teacher?" Elm asked.

"I think she said her name was Ms. Crow."

Mr. Underwood looked alarmed as Elm choked on his food and Sequoia growled.

"Dad! Why?" Willow cried out.

"Is there anything you need to tell me about this teacher?"

"No!" Elm and Willow said in unison.

"Are you sure?"

"What did she want, Dad?" Elm asked. "Why was she at the nursery?"

"She bought a couple of plants. She said she was your science teacher, and she wants you to study at the library, and neither of you have been going there. Didn't you tell me last week you were going to the library?"

"Yes, but something came up, and we didn't make it there," Elm said. "We'll start going there tomorrow." He nodded his head at Willow.

They left the table and went into the living room. Sequoia followed them.

"Are you okay?" Mrs. Underwood said.

"There was something very strange about that woman. I can't put my finger on it, but I hope I don't have any more encounters with her."

"Should we be worried about the children?" Mrs. Underwood asked.

"No, I think as long as Sequoia stays near them, they'll be okay." Mr. Underwood kissed his wife, then started clearing the table.

Together they went into the living room and watched television with Elm and Willow.

*****

Mr. Underwood's father had been aware of strange and unusual things happening in the past. He also knew portals to other worlds existed, but as far as he knew none had opened since his father had been a boy. Next time Elm and Willow stopped by for a visit, he would ask them about Ms. Crow.

Chapter 10

The Library

The next two weeks passed without any strange happenings. That didn't include Kyle, Roscoe, and Brody no longer attending school. It seemed like every third day someone was missing from class.

Elm, Willow, and Randy still had not been to the library, but today Ms. Crow loaded them down with homework. Most of it—research.

"Finally, we're going to the library," Randy said. "I've never been in a haunted house before."

"It's not haunted," Willow replied.

"Sure, it's not," Randy said.

When they stepped into the library, Randy gasped. Elm laughed as he watched Randy standing with his mouth open as he viewed the wide, elegant staircase. The staircase was the showcase of the library, and every eye was drawn to it upon stepping inside. The massive staircase, with its polished oak steps and black wrought iron rails, took you back to another time—Victorian days. Randy glanced from one side to the other, then up to the ceiling where a huge skylight allowed natural light to shine into the atrium onto the first floor. The walls had been removed and replaced with rows of bookshelves. The librarian's desk, which was enormous, was on the right-hand side as they came into the building. On the left side were rows of tables—some with computers. The outer walls were lined with bookcases full of books. There was a walkway around the upper two levels which also had thousands of books.

"This place is cool," Randy said. "The library in the city is big, but it's just a one-floor square building, and it's not haunted."

"Stop saying that," Willow said.

"Come on you two, let's get a table," Elm said.

Other students were coming into the library and grabbing the tables nearest the reference section. The reference section was in clear view of the front door and across from the librarian's counter. Several four- and six-seat tables were near the section because no one was allowed to check out reference books.

Elm set his backpack down at a table as Kobe and Juanita walked into the library.

They strolled toward Elm. "Mind if we share your table?" Kobe asked.

"There's always room for you," Elm said. "The more we work together, maybe the quicker we'll get done."

A Murder of Crows

They left the table and looked through the reference section. After selecting one book each, they began to look up information about carnivorous plants.

"Look." Elm pointed to a picture in his book. "There are over seven hundred species of carnivorous plants. This could take forever to list and describe all of them."

"We don't have to do it in one afternoon," Willow said. "We have all semester to study them, and Dad has books at the nursery we can check out."

They became quiet as they read their different books and wrote notes. Elm glanced over the top of his book when he heard the clicking of heels against the tile floor. Ms. Crow had entered the library. She stopped at the return books area even though she didn't have any books in her hands. She glanced around at the students. When she scanned over to where Elm and his friends were sitting, Elm quickly averted his eyes.

Heels clicked on the floor. Elm watched as Ms. Crow climbed the steps. She didn't stop on the second floor but continued on to the third floor.

Elm leaned over to Willow and whispered, "What's she doing here?" Willow shrugged her shoulders.

"Um, I need a break," Elm said. "I'm going to take a walk around."

"A break already," Kobe said. "You're not going to be very good as a study partner."

"Me too," Randy said. "I mean, I need a break."

Elm and Randy headed toward the wide staircase.

"I'll be back," Willow said to Juanita and Kobe.

"You know sometimes, you three act very strange," Juanita said.

Willow hurried up the steps behind Elm and Randy. "If we get caught, I'm telling Dad it was your fault."

"Shh!" Elm replied.

When they reached the third floor, they hid between a row of bookcases and watched Ms. Crow walk around talking to herself. She plucked a book from the shelf and turned it over in her hand but didn't glance at it. She turned away from the shelf and walked to the back wall. She glanced in all directions then stepped out of sight.

"Where did she go?" Randy asked.

The three of them rushed to the spot where she disappeared.

"This is where the door to the tower was originally," Elm said, "but when they remodeled the building, they sealed the tower closed."

"Maybe we all blinked at the same time and missed seeing her going back down the steps," Willow said.

"I don't think so, but let's get back downstairs before the others wonder what we're doing," Elm said.

After they sat back down, Kobe said, "Well, look who's back. Did you find anything interesting? I thought you were ghost hunting."

"No ghosts," Elm said. His pencil scratched across his paper as he continued to work on their assignments for the next hour.

A Murder of Crows

"Hey, Elm, isn't that your dog?" a boy sitting at another table said.

Elm turned toward the entrance. He watched in fascination as Sequoia lay flat on the floor and crept slowly past the librarian's desk. Once the dog was near the staircase, he leaped up the steps.

"Oh crap." Elm ran toward the dog.

"No running in the library," the librarian said.

Elm slowed down. Willow and Randy were not far behind. Elm heard Juanita talking to Kobe.

"Huh, there they go again," Juanita said. "I'm done for the day. Are you ready to leave?"

"Yes," Kobe replied.

Elm continued up the steps and found Sequoia on the third floor sitting next to the wall where Ms. Crow had disappeared.

"Did you find something?" he asked the dog.

Sequoia placed his paw against the wall and lightly scratched. Elm dropped to his hands and knees and searched along the wall. He looked up at Willow and Randy.

"I think there's an entrance into the tower. Do you see a door? I don't see a handle to open it."

Willow and Randy slid their hands along the wall and pushed at the same time. Elm heard a light click, and the wall opened one-fourth of an inch.

"What do you think you're doing!"

The three of them spun around. Standing less than a foot away from them was the twenty-two-year-old assistant librarian. She was thin and tall. Her blue hair stuck straight up like a punk rocker. She looked like she should be playing in a band instead of working in a library.

"Oh my gosh!" she said. "Is that a dog? You three need to leave now, and take that beast with you. And by the way you are banned from coming back for at least one week."

"Wait," Elm said. "Is there something behind this wall?"

She lifted her eyes. "Kids. Why do people have them?" Then looking back at Elm, she said, "The only thing behind that wall is the outside of the building."

Suddenly, a dark cloud covered the skylight, turning the inside to night and causing the bookshelves to cast long shadows against the wall.

The assistant looked up. "Not again."

Elm followed her gaze. It wasn't a cloud, but instead, hundreds of black crows sat on the skylight. He blurted out, "Thanks for all your help. We have to go. See you in a week."

They hurried down the steps and out the front door. The sky was bright and clear. No crows in the sky.

"That was creepy," Randy said.

"I know the tower room is behind that wall," Elm said. "We'll need to get back to the third floor soon and find out how to open the door."

They grabbed their bikes and sped home. Elm's skin crawled. The crows were watching—he couldn't see them, but he knew they were out there.

Chapter 11

Sequoia

Elm had heard the stories about Sequoia being an old dog from his grandfather. The story passed down from generation to generation in the Underwood family claimed that Sequoia had been the family protector since Elm's great-grandmother on his father's side of the family. She received the puppy as a present on her wedding day over one hundred years ago. Part Labrador, part golden retriever, and part unknown—but everyone believed he was every bit a magical creature. Sequoia was still the protector of the whole Underwood family, but he followed Elm and Willow everywhere they went. Sometimes unbeknownst to the children, he watched them from a distance. Especially now, since Ms. Crow had arrived in town.

Elm thought they were tall tales until the fiasco with the live oak tree's roots last month. Now Elm, Willow, and Randy knew the stories were true. Randy was the first person outside of the family to be included in the dog's history.

Sequoia usually slept at the foot of Elm's bed every night except twice a week when he slept in the bed with Willow. Tonight was one of those nights he was with Willow, but he wasn't sleeping.

He lay still and waited. He heard Elm banging around in his room. It was after midnight, and everyone else was asleep. Then he heard the static that a walkie-talkie makes when someone pushes the button. His ears perked up.

"Elm to Randy, are you there?" Elm spoke into the walkie-talkie. No immediate reply. "Randy, are you awake?"

"Uh-huh." Randy's sleepy reply came through the walkie-talkie. "I'll meet you out front in five minutes."

"Roger. Elm over and out."

Sequoia jumped off the bed, kicking Willow in the process. She sat straight up.

"Hey, that hurt," Willow said. "What's wrong? Do you need to go potty? Really? In the middle of the night."

A shadow passed Willow's door, and Sequoia scurried after it.

"What now?" Willow asked.

Elm eased the front door open, slipped out, and closed it before Sequoia caught up to him. The dog sat down and waited for Willow. She showed up seconds later and opened the door. Sequoia rushed out to where Elm and Randy stood on the porch. The dog had thought it was easy taking care of Elm and Willow until recently. If unnatural circumstances were happening, then Elm, Willow, and Randy were in the middle of it. Trying to protect them took a lot of energy.

"Elm, what are you up to?" Willow asked.

"We're on a mission," Elm said. "Why are you here?"

"I guess I'm on a mission too. Sequoia invited me when he jumped off the bed to follow you. So what's the mission?"

"We're going to the library and find out how to open the door to the tower."

"What! You're going to break into the library! What are Mom and Dad going to think when the police call them to pick us up from jail? This is not a good idea."

"No, not break in," Randy said. "I left a window in the back of the library open just enough not to be noticed but enough so we could push it up and climb through."

"Oh, that's so much better," Willow said sarcastically.

"You don't have to come with us," Elm said.

"Yes, I'm coming," she said. "I want to be there when the police arrest you two. Give me a minute. I need to change clothes."

Six minutes later, they jumped on their bikes and headed to town. Sequoia followed knowing this was not going to turn out well. When they arrived, they hid their bikes behind some bushes and followed Randy toward a window.

Randy shoved the window up, and one by one they silently climbed into the library. Sequoia ran toward the window and sprang through the opening. Sequoia, having great night vision for a dog, watched as the kids stumbled around in the dark. He rubbed against Elm, then walked beside him, leading Elm to the staircase. Suddenly, the sound of books hitting the floor stopped him in his tracks.

Sequoia growled low in his throat.

"What was that?" Willow whispered.

A child's crying floated down the steps. "I want to go home. I want my mommy."

"We need to leave," Randy said.

But instead of turning back to the window, Sequoia raced up the steps. Elm, Willow, and Randy followed him. When they reached the third floor, no one was there. The hidden door in the wall stood open. Again, Sequoia let out a low growl as he slinked into the room.

"What should we do?" Willow said.

"Let's go in," Elm replied.

The room was round with one window facing the front of the building. It had a chair and a few pieces of furniture, but what caught Elm's attention was an old tri-fold mirror that hung on the wall. The moonlight from the window bounced against it. The mirror shimmered.

"It looks like ripples on the water," Elm said.

"Do you think it's magical?" Willow asked.

"Where's the child we heard crying?" Randy glanced around the room.

Elm stepped forward and placed his hand against the mirror. Sequoia jumped through the mirror and disappeared. Thinking Elm would be right behind him, he sat down.

"No, no, no!" Elm cried. "Sequoia, come back!"

Sequoia sensed Randy pacing back and forth across the floor, and Willow's feelings of fright. He came back through the mirror.

"Don't ever do that again," Elm said.

"Let's go home," Willow demanded.

"Not yet. I have an idea." Elm smiled as his eyes widened.

Sequoia hated it when he got that look.

"Willow, you and Randy hold on to my pant loops and I'll stick my head through the mirror and see what's on the other side."

"Are you nuts!" Willow bellowed. "Another one of your great ideas."

Randy paced back and forth again. "We've been pulled through a portal without warning and hardly survived. We don't know what's on the other side of the mirror. Another world with trolls and manic trees? I'm not ready to try this."

Sequoia had watched Elm get into trouble since he was a baby. He knew as soon as Elm started bending forward, he would put his head through the mirror. He grabbed Elm by the seat of his pants so his whole body would not be sucked into the mirror.

"Elm! Stop!" Willow cried.

Elm pulled his head out of the mirror.

"What did you see?" Randy asked.

"There was a thick fog," Elm said. "I couldn't see anything."

Sequoia growled and backed toward the door. Cawing from crows came from the mirror. The dog whined.

"Okay," Elm said to the dog. "Let's get out of here before someone—or something—else comes through the mirror."

Terry Nolan

A Murder of Crows

Following Sequoia, they ran down the steps, climbed out the window, and pedaled their bikes home.

Yawning, Elm turned toward Randy. "Let's talk about this tomorrow."

Sequoia watched Elm rub his eyes as he crawled into bed. The dog went to Willow's room. She was already in bed with the covers pulled up to her chin. Sequoia returned to Elm's bed and slept the rest of the night there.

Chapter 12

Trouble

The next morning, they all overslept from their midnight adventure. When Elm boarded the school bus, the driver stood with his hands on his hips and an ugly glare on his face.

Elm got blasted by the driver. "This is the last time young Mr. Underwood. Not only are you late, but now your sister and friend can't make it to the bus on time either. I will report this to the principal."

Elm hung his head.

"Sorry, Mr. Loomis, we—" Willow started to apologize.

"I don't want to hear your excuses. The three of you make me late on my bus route, which in turn gets me into trouble. Now it's your turn to take the blame for my tardiness."

As Willow started to sit down next to Juanita, her friend picked up her backpack and set it on the seat next to her not even looking up. Elm shocked at what he was watching, waved to Willow to sit with them. He squeezed next to Randy to make room for her.

A Murder of Crows

"Wow," Willow whispered. "What's wrong with Mr. Loomis? He's never said a mean word the whole time he's been our driver."

"He's just fed up with Elm being late," Randy said.

"SHUT UP!" Mr. Loomis bellowed. "I want complete silence on this bus."

"I think there is more to this than Mr. Loomis being frustrated," Elm whispered.

All the students on the bus turned toward Elm. One boy called out, "Put a sock in it, Underwood."

An uneasy stillness filled the air during the ride to school.

When the bus turned into the driveway of the school, Principal Yost stood on the curb greeting students with a smile.

"That looks like a good sign," Willow whispered. "Mr. Yost is in a cheerful mood."

Or was he?

Elm, Willow, and Randy, the last three to get off the bus, smiled at the principal until—

Mr. Yost moved toward them. Towering more than a foot over all three of them, he growled. "You three have detention. Elm, follow me to my office."

Elm took a deep breath and opened his mouth.

"Don't say a word," Mr. Yost said.

Elm's shoulders slumped and he followed the principal into the school.

"Gee, how did Mr. Yost know we were in trouble?" Randy asked Willow. "I didn't see the bus driver call him." Elm could barely hear their conversation.

"I don't understand what's going on," Willow said, "but let's get to class before we're late and in more trouble."

Elm sat outside the principal's office in a very uncomfortable chair. He looked out the windows into the hallway. When the bell rang to indicate class was over, Willow and Randy came by and peeked through the glass. Elm shrugged his shoulders and held out his hands. Willow smiled and gave him a thumbs up. Randy waved. They left to go to their next class.

Mr. Yost came out of his office. "Come in."

Elm walked into the office and waited for the principal to tell him to take a seat. He sat down in a bulky chair with a worn-out cushion. His butt sank into the chair, bringing his knees almost to his shoulders. When Elm leaned back, the chair became unsteady, as if one leg was shorter than the other. The fabric was scratchy against his legs. The principal sat behind a huge desk covered with stacks of paperwork and a few family photos. Elm realized Mr. Yost's eyes were glazed over.

"Now that Kyle and his friends are no longer attending school here, I guess you've decided to become the school's troublemaker," Mr. Yost said.

"Where's Kyle?" Elm asked.

He saw Mr. Yost's mouth moving, but the screaming voice in his head belonged to Ms. Crow.

"The crows and plants ate him and his friends!"

Startled, Elm pushed back against the chair, which caused it to tumble over, and he rolled onto the floor.

A Murder of Crows

"Are you hurt?" Mr. Yost asked.

Elm realized the principal was standing over him with his hand held out to help him up. When he stood up, he noticed Mr. Yost's eyes were no longer glazed over.

"I hope our little talk has encouraged you to wear your watch so you will no longer be late for the bus or classes." Mr. Yost placed his hand on Elm's back and scooted him out of the office. "Don't be late for your next class." He chuckled.

Elm raced down the hall to the boys' room. He flung the stall door open, bent over, and threw up. His only thoughts were about Kyle being eaten. Washing his hands and wiping his face, Elm was glad no one had entered the bathroom while he was in it. He realized it was time for science class. He had missed lunch. *How long was I in the principal's office? It seemed like minutes, but half the day is gone. Had I been asleep?* He didn't think so.

Elm entered the classroom and started toward his desk when Ms. Crow clamped her hand around the back of his shirt and stopped him. "No, Mr. Underwood, you have a new desk. You will now be sitting in Kyle's old seat."

Everyone in the classroom said, "Ooh!"

Ms. Crow talked the whole class period. She seemed excited about a new hybrid plant she had created—a cross between a pitcher plant and a Venus flytrap. She explained that sometimes bugs were able to escape from the flytrap before it snapped shut. Now there would be no escape. The sticky substance of the pitcher plant would now be part of the Venus plant. She was almost giddy talking about the death of insects and small mammals. Again, Elm thought about Kyle and his friends.

The bell rang. Once Ms. Crow excused the class, Elm was first out the door. While waiting for Randy, Kobe walked past him. "Hey, Kobe—"

"Don't talk to me," Kobe muttered. "Who knew you would be the school's troublemaker?"

Elm's jaw dropped.

Willow dashed down the steps and met up with Randy and Elm. "What happened in the principal's office?"

"I don't know. It was like I was in a daze, but Mr. Yost seemed friendly when I left him." Elm looked over his shoulder. "Is there a sign on my back that says Pick on Elm Day?"

"I'm not sure what's happening, but the whole school seems to be whispering and gossiping about you," Willow said. "And not in a good way."

"Let's just get this day over with," Randy said. "We still have to get through detention."

The rest of the day flew by, then they headed to the principal's office, and Mr. Yost said, "Something urgent has come up. I don't have time today for your detention. I'll see you three tomorrow." He walked back into his office and slammed the door shut.

"Hurry, we can still catch the bus," Elm said.

They bolted out the front door, and when they were within three feet of the bus door, Mr. Loomis closed the door and pulled away from the curb.

A Murder of Crows

"Hey, wait for us," Randy yelled.

The kids on the bus—all smiling—waved goodbye.

"Unbelievable," Elm said. "Willow, call Mom and tell her Mr. Loomis left us behind on purpose."

Willow pulled her phone from her pocket and dialed. "Mom, we decided to go to the library before we come home. Can you or Dad pick us up in about an hour?"

"I'm hungry," Elm cried out. "I missed lunch."

"Yes, I'll tell him. Oh, tell Randy's parents he's with us. Okay. See you then." Willow hung up.

"Why did you tell her that? Why didn't you tell her we were left behind?"

"Calm down. I don't know what's going on, but I have to agree this has been a very strange day. We don't want to get Mom or Dad involved. I think it all has to do with Ms. Crow, and we don't want her doing anything to our parents or Randy's."

"You're right," Elm agreed.

"Mom also said we could go by the café and get something to eat and let them know she'll pay when she comes to pick us up," Willow said.

"What are we going to do at the library?" Randy asked.

"We're going back to the third floor and see if the secret door is still open, then we're going to go eat."

They left the school yard and headed to the library. Elm was so focused on climbing the steps and reaching the third floor, he didn't notice who else was in the library. Lucinda stood at the checkout counter as they walked past her.

Rushing to the hidden door, Elm came to a sudden stop. Ms. Crow appeared from around a bookcase. "How strange to see the three of you here. I thought the assistant librarian banned you for at least a week. Shall I call her and ask her if she retracted her statement?"

Standing as tall as he could, Elm replied, "No, Ms. Crow, that won't be necessary. We're leaving."

Outside, Randy said, "I don't want to do that again. She is one scary woman. When are we going to talk about you know what—what you saw through the mirror?"

"I'm starving," Elm said. "I missed lunch. We'll talk later." His growling stomach was the only thing on his mind at the moment.

Chapter 13

Into the Woods

The waitress came bustling over to the booth where Elm, Willow, and Randy were seated.

"Hi, Ms. Judith," Willow said. "My mom said to put our bill on her credit card."

"Sure, hon." While she took their order, the local middle school students sitting nearby all stood up and shifted to another table farther away. "Is there something I should know before I serve you? Do you kids have the cooties or maybe lice? I know." She smiled. "It's some type of childhood disease?"

Elm looked over the back of the booth and saw all the children sitting at a round table. They had their heads down and were murmuring to each other.

"Just a misunderstanding," Elm said. When Ms. Judith walked away, he sighed. "What is wrong with everyone? What have I done?"

"Did you hear what they just said?" Randy asked.

"No, Mr. Wolff, please tell us," Willow said sarcastically. "You're the one with hearing so perfect you can catch sounds half a mile away."

"Don't act so snooty, as if I'm different from you." Randy huffed. "You two talk to trees."

"Stop!" Elm said. "We can't be fighting with each other. Randy, what did they say?"

"They think you did something to Kyle and his friends. They're saying you want to become the next town bully."

"Are they nuts? Kyle and his friends could easily beat me in a fight. How can I be a bully?"

Judith brought their food to the table. As usual Elm had a chocolate milkshake with his meal. He was so hungry, he stopped talking and ate.

A car horn sounded outside.

"Mom's here," Elm said. "Let's go. I can't wait to get home. Randy, why don't you come over this evening and we'll talk about the library."

Three hours later, Elm, Willow, and Randy sat in the Underwood living room. Elm shuffled cards then dealt them out. They were playing poker—or pretending to play. No one looked at the cards in their hands.

"What did you see?" Randy said.

"I told you, I didn't see anything," Elm said. "There was a thick fog, but I heard the little girl crying for her mom. I thought I heard other people yelling, but I'm not sure. I heard crows cawing and an old lady cackling."

"You sure heard a lot to have had your head in the mirror for only two seconds," Randy said.

"It was all happening at the same time."

"What do you think we should do?" Randy asked.

"We have to go into the mirror," Elm said.

"No!" Willow replied.

"No!" Randy exclaimed.

"I think I have an idea," Elm said. "We can tell our parents that Ms. Crow has made arrangements with the library for the sixth- and seventh-grade science classes to have a weekend retreat. The event will take place this coming Friday and Saturday. That way we will have an excuse to be missing over the weekend." Elm smiled.

"Are you hard of hearing?" Willow asked. "We said no to going into the mirror."

Ignoring her, Elm continued, "I'll make a list of everything we'll need, including mosquito spray."

"I'm leaving." Randy stood up. "You're not listening to us. I'll see you at the bus stop tomorrow bright and early. We can't afford to be late." He laid his cards on the table and left the house.

Elm gathered up the cards and placed them back into the box. He left Willow sitting in the living room and went to his bedroom. He sat at his desk with a pen and paper before him. Yawning several times, he put his head on the table. He felt Sequoia tugging on his pant leg. Glancing down, he was surprised nothing was there, and the dog was on the bed sleeping. He stood up, stretched, and walked around the room. The house was quiet—too quiet. Restless with thoughts of the mirror running through his mind, he decided to go for a walk. He put his cap on and grabbed a flashlight then went out the back door. Sequoia jumped off the bed and trotted behind him. Standing at the boundary line that separated the backyard from the forbidden forest, he turned on the flashlight and peered into the darkness that swallowed the beam of light. He took a step across the line. The dog didn't follow.

"Come," Elm said. The dog lay down and whined. "Sequoia, I can't go into the woods without you."

The dog stood up, turned, and raced back to the house.

"Good grief, even my best friend has abandoned me." Elm wanted to turn and race back to the house, too, but something was forcing him to continue into the forest. He took several steps then stopped to scan the area. In the past month, the path had changed a lot, or did it just seem that way because it was dark and he was afraid? At least there was a full moon, and light flickered through the leaves of the trees.

"Can you help me find my way?" Elm asked, hoping the trees would reply…Silence.

"First, everyone at school turned against me, now my dog and the trees. What's going on?" He ran his hand through his hair, sweat dripping down his neck.

Something rubbed against his leg. His scream instantly faded into the thick, humid air. He shined the light at the ground, but the only things around him were bushes that partly covered the path. He shuffled along, barely picking up his feet. The trees grew closer together, blocking the moon's glow. Elm's foot tangled in a root. He flailed his arms and tumbled to the ground. He leaped up. The flashlight flickered, then went out.

"No! What am I doing? I'll never find my way." His heart pounded in his chest.

The deep voice of the live oak tree vibrated through the trees. "You're almost here. Keep walking."

Trembling, he took a few more steps and walked into the clearing in the middle of the forest. The moonlight returned, and the giant live oak tree loomed before him. Exhausted, he sat down with enough distance between him and the tangle of tree roots so the roots could not wrap around his ankles.

"What brings you into my woods in the middle of the night?" the live oak tree asked.

"I need your help," Elm said.

"I'm not here to help you, but since you made this treacherous journey, I will listen to what you have to say."

Elm tried to push the fear out of his voice. "There's a teacher…people are missing. I found a mirror. It's a portal to another land. I need to find the missing people." Tears ran down his cheeks. "Should I go through the mirror? Do you know what's on the other side?"

"That's a choice you have to make. The missing people are of no concern to you. If you go through the mirror, you will be lost to this side, and death most likely awaits you on the other side."

Elm yawned. His eyes grew heavy. "But what can I do?" Another yawn.

The live oak tree did not reply.

Chapter 14

A Change of Mind

The next morning Elm woke up in his bed. "It was a dream—a very vivid dream, but only a nightmare," he said to himself.

When he threw the bed covers off, he saw the sheets were littered with leaves and dirt. He rushed to the bathroom and looked in the mirror. Twigs were tangled in his hair and grime covered his face.

A knock on the door and Willow's voice asked, "Can I come in?"

He raced across the room and leaned against the door so she couldn't open it. "No, I'm not dressed. I'm getting ready to take a shower."

"Okay, I'll see you downstairs." Her footsteps receded down the hall.

Shaking all over, Elm took a deep breath as he stepped into the tub to take his shower. The warm water pounded against his skin, removing the dirt. The tension drained from his body. Back in his room, he hurriedly dressed and bounded down the steps to the kitchen.

He grabbed a piece of toast, two slices of bacon, and his backpack. "I'm not going to be late today," he said as he rushed out the door.

Willow and Randy stood at the end of the drive. When Elm arrived, Randy asked, "Did you make a list?"

"A list?" Elm tilted his head and squinted his eyes.

"Yes, the list of equipment we'll need for our new adventure. Willow and I talked on your walkie-talkie last night, and we agreed to go through the mirror."

"You talked on the walkie-talkie?" Elm asked.

"Are you going to repeat everything I say?" Randy laughed.

Elm stared from Randy to Willow and back.

"Your walkie-talkie was squalling away last night while you were sound asleep," Willow said. "I came into your room and answered Randy's call. We talked while you snored."

"I was in the bed?" Elm asked.

Willow's eyes widened. "What's wrong with you this morning? Of course, you were in bed. Where else would you be in the middle of the night?"

Elm shook his head. How could he be in bed and the woods at the same time? "I've been considering what you said yesterday, and I agree with both of you. We shouldn't go into the mirror."

"What!" they said in unison.

"You're right—it's too dangerous. We don't know what's on the other side, and we're just kids. We should tell Dad or some other adult. Who are we to try to outsmart a witch?"

"Elm—" Willow started to speak.

The bus pulled up, and Elm turned and climbed up the steps.

"Good morning." Mr. Loomis sounded like his old self…happy.

"You're in a good mood," Elm said.

"Of course, I am," Mr. Loomis said. "I thought I was always a ray of sunshine."

They walked toward an open seat. When Willow walked past Juanita, her friend said, "Hey, where are you going? Aren't you going to sit with me?"

Willow stopped. "Yesterday you…never mind." Willow sat down.

Elm glanced at his sister and shrugged. He and Randy sat down together a few seats behind Willow. No one on the bus seemed to pay them any attention. Everyone was laughing and talking.

"I wonder what's changed since yesterday?" Randy said.

"I don't know, but I'm glad we're not getting the evil eye today."

"We need to talk about why you changed your mind about the mirror," Randy said.

"Not now," Elm replied. "Later, when no one's around."

A Murder of Crows

When he stepped off the bus everything felt different. The sun's brilliant glow lit up the blue sky. No clouds and no crows. Even the leaves on the trees seemed to giggle.

Kobe stood on the sidewalk watching them.

"What are you waiting for? Another fight?" Elm grumbled.

"Huh?" Kobe lifted his head.

"Yesterday, you were mean and hateful," Randy said.

"To tell you the truth, I don't even remember yesterday," Kobe said.

They entered the school and settled into their seats in homeroom. Everyone was quiet in anticipation of Ms. Crow appearing at any minute. Click, click, click. High heels against the tile floor could be heard coming nearer with every step. The door opened and Ms. Crow—no, Ms. Yang walked in. Tiny and petite, with a smile on her face, she said, "Good morning, Ms. Crow is taking a day off, and I will be your substitute teacher."

Elm was glad he wouldn't have to deal with Ms. Crow today, but he wondered where was she and was she up to no good.

The bell rang.

The day went smoothly. No arguments, no bullying, no crows on the windowsill, and no Ms. Crow. It was a great day until—

The crackle of the microphone through the speaker interrupted the last class of the day. Mr. Yost's voice said, "Elm Underwood, report to the principal's office."

"Oh no," Elm said as he grabbed his backpack and slowly walked out of the classroom. He met Willow outside the office door. "Did the principal call you too?"

"It's probably about detention. Where's Randy?"

"He didn't call for Randy," Elm said.

They walked into the office together. Sequoia sat in the middle of the room.

"Is this your dog?" Mr. Yost asked.

"Yes," they both replied.

"He won't leave. He's been here for the past thirty minutes, whining and howling. It almost sounds like he's talking. Get him out of here."

Elm walked toward Sequoia, but the dog backed up. He placed his front legs down, his butt in the air, and raised his head to let out a howl. Except it didn't sound like a howl. It sounded like "Daaaad!"

Willow rushed over and got down on her knees. "What did you say?"

Again, the dog howled, "Daaaad!"

Ignoring Mr. Yost and anyone else in the office, Elm said, "We have to go home. Go get Randy out of class."

"Excuse me," Mr. Yost said.

"Sorry, we have to go." Elm and Sequoia went outside and waited for Willow and Randy.

Chapter 15

Dad

Five miles home. They ran, they walked, and they ran some more. They stopped at the nursery. It was the middle of the afternoon in late September. Not many customers were buying plants because they were waiting for the big sale that happened every year on the first of October.

"Is our dad here?" Elm asked the cashier.

"No," she replied.

Willow waited for a second then said, "Has he been here today?"

"Yes, he was here this morning, but he didn't look like he felt well. About an hour later, he told me that he forgot some paperwork at home, and he needed it. He then left the store, and I haven't seen him since."

Out the door they flew and continued home. They busted through the front door, slamming it open so hard it made a dent in the wall.

"Mom! Mom," Elm yelled.

Willow hurried up the stairs. Randy and Sequoia followed Elm through the kitchen and out the back door. Willow returned, and they looked toward the garden.

"Look, there she is pulling weeds." Randy pointed.

As they walked toward her, a lump formed in Elm's throat. Mrs. Underwood glanced up as they approached.

"Oh no," Elm cried.

Mrs. Underwood's eyes were glazed over. She dug up plants and threw them in a compost pail. The scent of fresh strawberries filled the air.

"Mom," Willow said. "Where's Dad?"

She laid down her trowel and slid her mud-covered fingers through her hair, then she stood up. "Your dad? Isn't he at work?"

"Your dress…it's ripped, and you have blood on your face," Elm said.

"There were several blackbirds in the garden when I came out. I tried to shoo them away. They landed on my shoulders, and I swear they tried to lift me up. I hit them with the spade, and they flew away. I guess besides tearing my dress they must have scratched my face." She squatted back down and started pulling up more vegetables.

"Elm's jaw dropped open, then he said. "Let's check the barn." The large building was filled with arborist equipment—several rope wrenches, harnesses, pruning gear, saws, and an ATV with an attached wagon. They stood in silence at the entrance. Scattered on the floor lay black crow feathers.

A Murder of Crows

Willow crouched down for a closer look. Small holes were in the sawdust. "Are those holes made from high heels?" Answering her own question, she said, "Ms. Crow's been here."

"We have to get to the library now," Elm said.

"What about Mom?" Willow asked. "We need to take her into the house and get her cleaned up before we leave."

"It may be too late for Dad if we don't hurry," Elm said.

Randy stepped between them. "Wait. First, I want to know why you changed your mind this morning about going into the mirror."

Elm took a deep breath. "I don't know if I was dreaming or if it really happened, but the live oak tree told me if I went into the mirror, I would never return. But now that ugly witch has taken Dad, and nothing is going to stop me from going after him."

"We'll all go," Randy said, "but we need to have a plan, or the tree may be correct, and we could be stuck in another realm. You need to finish making the list you started the other day of items we'll need. Willow, you should help your mom in the house and make her comfortable. I have to come up with an excuse to tell my parents as to why we're not going to be around this weekend."

Elm reluctantly agreed, and they left the barn going in three different directions.

Two hours later, they met in the Underwood's kitchen with backpacks bulging.

"What did you tell your parents?" Willow asked.

"Actually, before I could tell them an excuse, they told me they were going away for the weekend. They wanted to ask your mom to take care of Bella, but I told them your dad would be on a business trip, and your mom wasn't feeling well."

"If they can't leave Bella, are they still going?" Elm asked.

"Yes, they'll drop Bella off at our grandparents' house," Randy said.

"Your parents usually go away for the weekend about every other month, don't they?" Willow said.

"Yeah, always when there's a full moon," Elm added.

"They say it's more romantic when there's a full moon. Yuck," Randy said.

Willow laughed.

"How's your mom?" Randy inquired.

"She seems to be stuck in whatever activity she's doing," Willow said. "When I returned to the garden, she was still digging in the dirt until I helped her up, then we went upstairs for her to shower. She didn't want to get out of the shower until I helped her out, dried her off, and got her in bed. She's now lying down and watching television."

They glanced at Elm. "Looks like I didn't need to make a list," he said. "You both have your backpacks full. What's in them?"

"I don't plan to starve on this adventure," Willow said. "I'm glad Mom buys our groceries in bulk. I packed two jars of peanut butter, a box of crackers, ten pouches of chicken, and ten pouches of tuna. I have some chocolate candy and cookies, also two bottles of water for each of us, and I hope we'll be able to find more water on the other side. Oh, and some dog food for Sequoia. I have my cell phone and my wand."

"Um, your wand?" Elm was confused.

"Yes, you never know if we'll have magical abilities or not, so I'm bringing it just in case magic exists there."

He glanced at Randy. "What do you have?"

With a gleam in his eyes, Randy called off the items. "I have two waterproof blankets, extra socks for all, matches, a flashlight with extra batteries, a Swiss army knife, and a hammer."

"A hammer?" Elm peeked into Randy's pack.

"Yep, you never know when you may need to hit a strange creature." Randy laughed.

"Okay, okay. I have ropes, and walkie-talkies. I don't think your cell phone will work, but you need to bring it along. Bug spray, compass, poncho, matches, and candles. We have sleeping bags that we can tie on top of our packs."

"We're ready, but how are we going to walk through the library without everyone asking us questions?" Willow said.

"I thought we'd go through the back window again," Elm said. "First, Randy will go into the library and open the window. Then we'll pass the backpacks through the window to him. Willow, you and I will climb into the building."

Willow and Randy shrugged their shoulders. Elm wasn't sure the plan would work but they had to try. They mounted their bikes. Elm wobbled at first with the load he carried, but once he got his balance, he pedaled as fast as he could. Sequoia ran alongside the bikes.

Chapter 16

Uninvited

Randy entered the library. It was late afternoon, and a few students were at the tables.

"Hey, Randy."

He glanced over and saw Lucinda, the girl with purple streaks through her blond hair, smiling at him. "Hey," he replied but didn't stop to talk. He continued to the back of the building where the restrooms were located. He made his way to the window, opened it, and then waved at Elm and Willow.

The window was next to a narrow staircase that would take them to the third floor. It was a stairway the maids would have used when the place was a home and not a library. Randy dragged the backpacks through the window. He then helped Elm and Willow in. Sequoia jumped in without any help.

"Wait here," Randy said. "I have to go back out the front entrance. Someone spotted me when I came in, and if I don't go back out, they might come looking for me."

"Good idea," Elm said. "But we'll carry this stuff up the steps. We don't want anyone to see us."

Lucinda was waiting by the checkout counter when Randy returned. "Are you leaving already?" she asked. "I thought you could sit at my table, and we could study together since you're by yourself. Come to think of it, I've never seen you without Elm tagging along."

"Um, thanks for the offer, but Elm's outside waiting for me." He turned and walked away.

*****

Lucinda watched Randy exit the building. She waited thirty seconds, then followed him. Coming out of the building, she looked around. Out of the corner of her eye, she caught a shadow moving. Randy darted around the edge of the building. She rushed over and peeked down the side of the building until she saw Randy take another turn to the back of the library. She hurried to follow him. She didn't see Elm anywhere. She drew in her breath when she saw Randy climbing through a window back into the library. What in the world was he up to?

She waited for forty seconds, pacing back and forth. She didn't want to run into him, but she didn't want to lose him either. She crawled through the window, scrapping her knee on the windowsill. She then tiptoed up the back staircase and slid behind a row of books. She watched as Elm hit the wall and a door opened. Elm, Willow, Randy, and that stupid dog hurried into the opening. They closed the door behind them.

Lucinda came out of hiding and stood next to the wall. She tapped it. Nothing happened. She pushed on it, but still the wall didn't budge. She kicked it and the door bounced open.

She rushed into the room and asked, "What are you doing?" She spun around. No one was in the room except her. She walked around, banging and kicking the walls to find another hidden door, but there was none. She noticed the antique tri-fold mirror trimmed in thin gold leaf that flaked off in places.

She stood in front of the mirror wondering how they could have disappeared. Suddenly a hand came out of the mirror wrapped around her wrist, and yanked her into the mirror. She screamed, but the sound wasn't heard by anyone in the library. She tumbled into a new world.

*****

Now there were four and Sequoia. They stood in a circle surrounded by a thick fog.

"Why are you following Randy?" Elm scowled.

Tears ran down her cheeks. "He was acting strange. I thought he might be in some kind of trouble, and I wanted to help him. But then I saw the three of you go through that hidden door. I needed to know what was behind it…wait, where are we?" Lucinda realized she was no longer in Oak

Valley. She trembled as she tugged at the neck of her shirt, terror filling the pit of her stomach.

"Hope you didn't have any plans for the weekend," Willow said mockingly. "Or the rest of your life."

"Don't be so mean," Randy said. "She didn't asked to be pulled through the mirror."

"We couldn't let her go blabbing to everyone that we disappeared in the tower of the library," Willow said.

"Who do you think would believe her?"

"We don't want Ms. Crow to know we're here," Willow said.

"She probably has spies everywhere and already knows we're here." Randy growled.

"Stop arguing," Elm said. "She's here, and we have to deal with it."

They turned and faced Lucinda, who was still sitting on the ground.

"I'm sorry I followed you. I want to go home. How do I get back through the mirror?" Lucinda stood up and turned around. "Where is the mirror?"

"It's too late," Elm said. "The mirror is lost in the fog. You'll have to go with us."

"Go with you where?" Her hands shook as she placed one of them over her mouth to keep from screaming. Sequoia trotted next to her. Unaware of her actions, she automatically placed the fingertips of her other hand upon the dog's head and petted him.

A Murder of Crows

"Sit back down, and I'll tell you the short version of what's happening," Elm said.

Willow groaned, but everyone sat down. Sequoia laid his head on Lucinda's knee. The dog's presence comforted her.

"You know about all the people missing from school—Mr. Hardy, Kyle and his buddies, and a few other people. They were taken by Ms. Crow. Today she took our dad." Elm pointed toward Willow. "We're here to rescue him and anyone else she kidnapped."

"I thought Mr. Hardy left town, and Kyle and his gang were kicked out of school," Lucinda said. "Why would Ms. Crow take them?"

"Ms. Crow is a witch," Elm said, "and when you see her in this new land, you won't recognize her. She'll look like an old hag.

"Okay, let's say I believe you," she said. "Where are we? How do you plan to save these people and your dad? How will we get back home and when?"

"Good questions, no answers," Elm said.

At that moment, Sequoia growled. Elm placed his finger to his lips. "Shh."

A python-sized rattlesnake weaved through them. It stopped long enough to rattle its tail, then slipped into an area of tall grass.

"That was one humongous rattlesnake," Randy said. "I wonder what other creatures lurk around here."

The fog lifted. A light breeze whispered through the tall grasses surrounding them, causing it to sway back and forth as if it were dancing to the sound of music. Colorful butterflies darted around flowers near them. Across the way, they could see a swarm of mosquitoes, but for now, they kept their distance. To the left lay a sandy path that curved out of sight.

"It's really kinda beautiful here," Willow said.

Elm slid his fingers over the grass. "You know this type of grass usually grows in prairies."

How do you know so much about plant life?" Randy asked.

Willow laughed. "When he's not causing trouble or hanging around you, he has his head in the computer researching information about trees, plants, and environments."

Randy looked at Elm. "You've never mentioned that to me."

"I want to study environmental science when I go to college," Elm said.

"What's wrong with you?" Lucinda looked from one to the other. "We're in another world. We're never going to go to college or even back to school. I don't understand why none of you are upset or frightened."

"Calm down, Lucinda," Randy said. "Everything will be fine, and we'll probably be back home within two days." He pulled a blanket from his backpack and handed it to her. "It's time to rest. We'll have a long day tomorrow."

"Hmmp." She took the blanket, spread it out on the ground, and lay down.

The sun slowly hid behind the tall grass and the bullfrogs began to croak their songs.

Chapter 17

Pooka

Elm yawned as he squinted at the sky. It looked like a painter's canvas. The sun hid behind the wisps of clouds as they flowed across the sky in many colors. There were dramatic pinks, light and dark blue clouds, and in the distance large, long-legged egrets winged across the heavens. At least that's what he thought they were. As long as they weren't crows.

He glanced around. Everyone was still asleep except Sequoia. The dog seemed to always be on sentry duty.

Sequoia trotted next to Elm, laid his head in his lap, and closed his eyes for a few seconds. Elm whispered soothing words to the dog while he stared at the sandy path wondering what they would encounter once they started their journey.

Lucinda jerked awake, sat straight up, and waved her hands around her head. "Ouch! Something bit me."

Willow and Randy both woke up scratching. Elm reached into his bag and pulled out the bug spray.

"I guess the mosquitoes finally found us." Elm sprayed himself then passed the can around.

"Oh my gosh, I thought I was having a bad dream, but I see it wasn't a dream. I'm here with you. We really came through a mirror. What's next? A rabbit with a watching yelling he's late?" Lucinda took the can of spray and misted herself with it.

"Let's eat and get moving. We're out in the open, and I don't like it." Willow pulled the crackers and peanut butter out of her pack. She prepared two cracker sandwiches for each person. They sat in a circle. A long snake crawled through them. They sat still and waited for the snake to continue on its way. It stopped, lifted its head, swiveled it around, then dropped back down and slithered away.

"That was weird," Elm said. "The snake acted like he wasn't expecting to see anyone. Then when he saw us, he got scared and couldn't get away fast enough."

"I think you're seeing things," Randy said. "We surprised it, and it hurried off."

After the small meal, they packed everything up and started their journey. Once they rounded the curve, the tall grass grew only on the right side. On the other side, small, twisted, and contorted oaks, pines, and cedars formed a forest. Most of the trees were covered with knots and lumps making them look like old ladies bent over with warts and bruises.

"Those trees look like trees I've only seen in fantasy books." Randy said. "and usually something creepy is roaming in them."

"They look like trees that grow near the coast where the wind always blows which doesn't allow them to grow upward," Elm said. "But there are some I don't recognize."

They continued along the trail, constantly looking all around for anything that would be considered abnormal. Elm stayed alert and glanced at Randy every once in a while to see if he had heard or smelled anything.

Randy stopped and cocked his head.

"What is it?" Elm asked.

"Not sure. Sounds like a lot of animals scurrying through the fallen leaves."

Suddenly, a huge rabbit hopping on its back legs crossed in front of them and into the grass.

"There's a rabbit." Lucinda squealed. "Did he have a watch?"

"Don't be silly." Willow scowled. "We're not in wonderland."

Something snapped, then there was a groan. The grass swayed as if there were a fight going on beneath it. Then everything grew quiet, and a boy about four feet tall emerged onto the path. He had white hair and gray eyes. He wore a white short-sleeve shirt and gray pants. He didn't wear shoes. His feet were not human—they were rabbits' feet.

He stared at the group on the path, then said, "Hello."

"Who are you?" Elm asked.

"I'm Finn," the boy replied. "Who are you?"

"I'm Elm." He pointed to each person as he introduced them. "This is my sister, Willow. My best friend, Randy, my dog, Sequoia, and an uninvited person, Lucinda."

Terry Nolan

A Murder of Crows

"Why are you in here? This is quite a band of humans to be marching around without a guide. No telling what kinda trouble you might run into." Finn pulled a blade of grass and started eating it.

"Are you the rabbit we saw run across the path?" Willow asked.

"I don't know what you saw, so how would I know if I were the rabbit you saw?" Finn laughed.

"Okay, what are you?" Willow asked.

"I'm a pooka."

"What's a pooka?" Elm asked.

"A shape-shifter," Finn said. "I can become a rabbit, dog, horse, or other animals. I'm part of the fae family."

"Fae?" Willow asked. "Is the Fairy Kingdom, I mean Queendom, here? Do you know the fairy queen, Marcelina?" Willow had met Queen Marcelina in the fairy Queendom last month when they had been pulled underground. The fairies had helped them along their way.

"There's no kingdom here," Finn said. "Only grasses, forests, lots of mud, and the river."

"Wait a minute." Elm walked a few feet away from Finn. "We need to talk," he said to the others. They followed him, except for Sequoia, who rubbed up against Finn.

"This is exciting," Lucinda whispered. "A real live fairy. I didn't know they existed."

"What's the matter?" Willow glanced back over her shoulder at Finn.

"Just because he is part fairy doesn't mean we can trust him. There are good and bad fae." Elm turned and raised his voice. "Finn, how did you know we were here?"

He laughed. "The snake told me."

"The snake can talk?" Randy said.

"The snake is a pooka," Finn said. "Not always a nice one, but he is what he is. When he saw strangers here, he rushed to me and told me. I came to check you out."

"I don't trust him," Elm whispered.

"It looks like Sequoia does," Randy said. "I think we should give him a chance. Maybe he can help us find the hag."

"I agree with Randy," Willow said.

Elm walked back to where Finn waited. "It seems like Sequoia likes you. That's a good sign that we should trust you. I'll tell you why we're here. We're looking for an old hag."

Finn giggle. "There are a few old hags around here."

"This one," Elm continued, "came to our town. She changed herself to a beautiful woman and pretended to be a teacher."

Finn cocked his head to the side.

"She stole people from the town and probably brought them here. The last person she took was my dad, and I'm here to get him back."

"What else can you tell me about her?" Finn asked.

"She likes plants that eat bugs, and there are always crows around her. I think she controls them."

"Crows!"

Elm heard a loud *pop,* and Finn disappeared.

Chapter 18

The Journey Begins

"Well, a lot of help Finn turned out to be," Elm said. "I think we should stay in the woods but keep the path in sight." He looked over his shoulder to see if anyone—or thing—was behind them.

After they'd been walking and stumbling over tree roots, Lucinda, not used to hiking in the woods, said, "I'm going to the path. You guys can stay in the woods if you want, but I'm tired of tripping." She trudged over to the pathway.

Elm wondered for a second, then agreed. "I guess we could get back on the path. I haven't seen a crow or any other type of bird flying overhead."

"Do you even know where we're going?" Willow asked.

"I think we should keep heading in this direction. If we go back, we'll just end up back at the library."

Leaves and ivy covered the tangled roots of trees, making it difficult not to trip as Elm stomped toward the path. He saw Lucinda several yards ahead of him. She hadn't waited for any of them to catch up. Suddenly, the sun disappeared as crows the size of condors filled the sky. Sequoia barked. Elm, Willow, and Randy leaped back under the trees.

Elm cried out, "Lucinda, hide!"

She turned halfway around and ran as fast as she could, but the largest of the crows plunged downward and snagged her jacket with its talons before she could reach the safety of the trees. She screamed as the bird pulled her off the ground. Elm rushed out of the trees and grabbed her legs. He hoped the extra weight would hold her down. Willow pulled her wand from her pack and pointed it, but there was no magic in this land. The bird was strong. It raised both Lucinda and Elm off the ground. Randy vaulted toward Elm, gripping Elm's legs and adding additional weight to hold them both down.

Elm heard the crow's caw, caw when suddenly the bird's voice was cut short when, from out of nowhere, an arrow flew overhead and hit the crow in the heart, killing it instantly. Its talons loosened their grip as the bird fell to the ground. Elm had been pulling with all his strength, and the sudden release from the bird caused them all to tumble into the grass. They were well hidden in the tall grassland.

Lucinda whimpered as she pulled off her jacket.

"Are you hurt?" Willow asked.

"No," Lucinda said. "That awful bird didn't get its claws in my skin, but look at my poor jacket. It's shredded, and I've only had it a month."

Willow smiled. "I'm glad you're okay. Sorry about your coat."

A Murder of Crows

Elm lifted his head. No crows insight, but where had the arrow come from?

Still lying in the grass, Elm began to shake. He wasn't trembling from fear but from vibrations coming from the ground.

Randy crawled over to Elm. "Do you feel it? Something's coming. Do you think the horses with fire are here? We don't have anywhere to hide." They had encountered fire horses when they were underground. The horses turned out to be very dangerous animals.

Elm heard the thunderous hooves pounding against the earth. The sound of the hooves became muffled as they trotted onto the sandy path. Sequoia leaped out of the grassland. Elm held his breath, waiting…Would the dog be burned or kicked to the side like the last time he encountered the horses? Sequoia finally let out a friendly bark, not a growl.

A deep voice sounded. "Hello, dog. Who's there? Come out into the open."

Elm stood up and walked between the reeds of grass. The others waited to see what would happen. He gasped as he saw twenty centaurs meandering on the path.

Willow and Lucinda stepped out of the grass, followed by Randy. As soon as Randy stepped onto the path, the centaurs backed farther away. They whispered among themselves, and their hooves pawed the ground.

The one centaur that seemed to be the leader had a young man's face with deep-set brown eyes. His long black hair hung down his back like the mane of a horse.

A Murder of Crows

Lucinda, being a person who said what she thought, blurted, "Oh my gosh, you're gorgeous."

The leader ignored her and kept his eye on Randy. He lifted his head and sniffed the air. Facing Randy, he asked, "What are you?"

"I'm a boy—a human boy," Randy said.

"You don't smell like the rest. Your scent is strong. Your blood is mixed. It's part human and part wolf."

"Oh no, here we go again," Randy said. "My last name is Wolff, but I am not a wolf."

Lucinda stood next to Randy. She sniffed his neck. "Smells like a boy who needs a bath." She laughed.

The centaur turned to Elm. "There aren't any humans here, so why are you traveling through my territory?"

"I'm Elm, and this is my sister, Willow. That's my friend Randy, and the girl is Lucinda. We're searching for an old hag who surrounds herself with crows. She's kidnapped people from our world, including my father. We're here to take them back. Do you know where we can find her?"

"My name is Berthold. I'm the ruler over all of the centaurs. This is a very dangerous mission you're planning. The old hag lives across the river on an island. I've never heard of anyone who has gone to the island ever returning. Are you sure you want to take this journey? I suggest you go back to wherever you came from."

"We can't turn back," Elm said.

"I'll be glad to go home," Lucinda said. "Can you take me there?"

"Shut up." Willow stepped in front of Lucinda.

"How far is the river?" Elm asked.

"For us, about an hour's gallop," Berthold said, "but for you, with short legs and tiny feet, I'd say three or four hours."

"I don't suppose you could help us get there any faster?" Elm asked.

"Sorry, young Elm. We have no qualms with the old hag, and we want to keep it that way. We mind our own business, and she doesn't bother us. Just follow the path. Once you arrive at the river, a boatman will escort you to the island."

"How do we contact the boatman?"

"Don't worry. He'll know you're there."

"And the crows?" Randy asked.

"They'll be back to pick up their dead and take it home. You probably won't see them again for at least an hour." Berthold handed Elm a bow with seven arrows. "Make sure you hit your target." The centaurs turned and galloped out of sight.

Chapter 19

Take Cover

Already they had wasted several hours talking to Finn, running from crows, then encountering the centaurs. Willow suggested they eat again before they went any farther. They found a small clearing in the woods not far from the path. Sitting in a circle, Willow passed around a jar of peanut butter with a plastic knife, a pack of crackers, a bottle of water, and a cookie for everyone. She also had a plastic collapsible dog bowl. She filled it with water and put a medium amount of dog food on the ground.

"I don't understand. How did you know to pack all this stuff? And how do you stay so calm with all these strange creatures showing up?" Lucinda mumbled around her mouth full of peanut butter-covered crackers.

"We go camping a lot," Elm said.

"We've also seen some strange things in the forest behind our house," Willow said.

"Oh my gosh, you've been in the forest? You must have been in the forest. It was the three of you that found that missing family last month, right? I would never step foot in those woods. I don't even want to be here, but here I am in the middle of wonderland."

Hearing the caw of crows, they looked skyward. The crows circled around one crow. The one in the middle carried the dead crow in its talons. The birds cawed in unison as if they were singing a song. A few crows straggled behind the circle. When they flew over where Elm and Willow sat, the birds dropped their poop.

"Hey." Elm scooted across the ground. "They did that on purpose."

"Well, at least they're a bad shot, or we would have been covered," Willow said. "They're not small birds."

Randy rolled over laughing. "Those birds are so big it's like Sequoia dropping a pile on you."

"Eew, that's disgusting." Lucinda made a gagging noise like she was going to throw up.

Elm rose to his feet. "Let's get going before they come back."

They started at a good pace. The first hour passed with no problems. Content with their progress, Elm picked up a stick and threw it. Sequoia chased after it and brought it back. Elm and Sequoia played for a while as they walked. A cool breeze blew through the trees, and the temperature dropped a few degrees.

"Elm, what time is it?" Randy asked.

"It's one o'clock," he replied.

"It seems to be getting dark very early," Randy said.

At that moment a loud, violent clap of thunder rolled across the sky, shaking the trees. A downpour began to fall…not a downpour but a torrential rain. Veins of lightening ran across the sky, lighting up the clouds.

Soaked, Elm held tight to a waterproof blanket, trying to cover himself, but the wind whipped it out of his hands several times. He rushed to catch it before it blew away.

"What are we going to do now?" Willow bellowed. A loud boom of thunder shook the trees, drowning her out.

"We can't travel in this," Elm yelled as lightning struck a nearby tree.

"Look." Randy pointed. "There's a circle of boulders just up that hill. We should be safe there."

Elm braced himself against the rain and held onto the blanket and his backpack while the wind tried to rip everything out of his hands. Just past the boulders, he saw an opening to a cave. He pointed. They rushed into the entrance but stopped short once they were out of the rain.

"Do you think we'll be safe?" Lucinda asked.

"Safer than being beaten to death by the rain." Randy pulled a flashlight out of his bag and shined it around. "There's some wood. Maybe we can start a fire."

Lucinda, who hadn't helped do anything since the beginning of this adventure, gathered the wood and piled it in a campfire fashion.

Elm struck one of his matches, and to everyone's surprise, the fire lit quickly.

They huddled near the flame. Elm and Willow sat on one side, and Randy and Lucinda sat on the other side with their backs toward the wall so they could see if something came from inside or outside the cave. Sequoia lay at the entrance.

The rain lasted thirty minutes. The sun came out, and the heat from the sun mixed with the wet grass caused a mist to rise from the ground, making it hard to see two feet in front of them.

"I think we should go," Randy suggested.

"We can hardly see," Elm said.

"I smell a foul odor coming from inside the cave," Randy said. "Not sure what it is, but the scent is getting stronger. Whatever is causing it is coming closer."

Lucinda lifted her head and sniffed. "I don't smell anything."

Elm and Willow knew Randy had a very sensitive nose and usually could smell odors before anyone else. Sequoia let out a low rumble.

"Okay, grab your stuff—we're leaving." Elm kicked the wood to scatter it and stomped out the fire.

Into the mist they walked. Slowly, they found their way back to the path. After a half-hour, the sun burned the mist away. Elm's instinct told him someone—or thing—was following them, but when he looked around, he didn't see any signs of an intruder.

Suddenly, Randy froze and looked into the sky.

"What is it?" Elm whispered.

"I hear the cawing of the birds," he said.

A Murder of Crows

"Hurry into the woods," Elm said. "Everyone, squat down and pull the blankets over your head."

They scurried into the edge of the trees as Elm directed. Sequoia crawled next to Elm. With the dark blankets disguising their presence, the crows flew overhead and continued down the road.

"That was close," Elm said. "We need to hurry and find the river before the crows discover us."

"It won't take them long to return," Willow said.

Elm looked at Randy. "Keep an ear out for them. Every time you hear them, we'll go into the trees and cover ourselves until they're gone."

Randy quickly rolled up the blankets, and they continued down the trail. He handed one to Lucinda to carry, and he carried the other one. No one spoke a word.

"They're coming." Randy snatched the blanket from Lucinda and tossed it to Elm.

They scrambled under the trees and covered themselves with the blankets. Elm peeked out. The crows didn't fly away but landed on the sandy path. Elm held his breath. The birds no longer looked like crows, but more like vultures looking for a good meal. That was a frightening thought.

He pulled the bow off his shoulder and placed an arrow on it. Aiming, he let the arrow fly. He missed.

The crows, caw cawing, and scratching, side-stepped closer to the blankets. Sequoia growled and burst out of the trees, barking at the birds. A few of the crows flew upward, but one—a huge one—flew over, grabbing Sequoia and puncturing the dog's hindquarters with its talons. The bird lifted the dog in the air. Sequoia first yelped, then howled. He whimpered, then went silent.

"No!" Elm screamed. He shot another arrow at the crow, ripping its wing apart. The bird released Sequoia, and the dog fell silently to the ground.

Elm and Willow rushed to the dog. Willow laid Sequoia's head in her lap as tears slid down her cheeks. Elm bent over, laying his face gently against Sequoia's side, soaking the dog's fur with his tears and repeated, "I'm sorry I'm so sorry. I love you."

Randy flung the blankets around in the air until the crows finally left the area. He bolted over to Sequoia and sat down. Sniffing and wiping tears, he asked. "How is he?"

"I think he's dead or near death," Elm sobbed.

A *pop* came from a few feet away. Elm looked up and saw Finn.

"I can heal the dog," Finn said.

"Yes, yes, please help," Elm cried.

Finn laid his hands on Sequoia's bleeding skin and mumbled a few words under his breath. Sequoia lifted his head, whined, then licked Elm's and Willow's hands.

"Thank you," Elm said.

"Will he be all right?" Willow asked.

"Probably a little sore, but he'll recover." Finn smiled.

Randy folded the blankets and laid them under Sequoia's head.

"Have you been following us this whole time?" Elm asked.

A Murder of Crows

"Yes," Finn replied.

"I knew someone was watching us. Why didn't you show yourself?"

"I figured you didn't want me around since I did a disappearing act when we first met."

"So why are you following us?" Randy asked.

"I want to go to the island with you and help get your father and friends. When I was only five years old, the hag captured my dad in a snare. My dad had shifted into a fox. While frolicking around, he stepped into her trap. It broke his leg. The hag had no mercy. She chopped off his foot and took him to the island. I was able to transform into a bumblebee and followed them. I watched as she had a crow pick him up and drop him into the mouth of a giant carnivorous plant. Now I'm older, and I can change into many different things, and if I travel with you, I'll not be fighting this battle alone." Finn sat down and waited for their reply.

Sequoia stood up and limped over to Finn. He licked his face, then curled up beside him.

Elm, Willow, and Randy stepped away. Lucinda sat next to Finn and talked to him.

"How do you know you can trust him?" Randy asked.

"If his story is true, it's heartbreaking," Willow said.

"He saved Sequoia," Elm said. "Besides, what do we have to lose if he's with us? Maybe he can turn into something useful and guide us to the hag."

They ambled back to where Finn sat. "We've decided you can join us on our journey," Elm said.

Finn jumped up. "Woohoo! Finally, revenge for my father's death." He glanced at Sequoia. "You should give the dog at least an hour to rest, then he should be completely healed and can travel without any pain.

Elm sat next to Finn as they waited for Sequoia to heal. "Thanks again for helping," Elm said. "I never thought Sequoia would get hurt. I always thought it would be me, that would need to be rescued."

"You still may need to be saved. The battle hasn't started, yet," Finn said. "Why do you have a H on your cap?"

"The H stands for Hawks, its our school mascot. You know I've never told anyone before, but talking about being rescued, I've always thought some day a hawk would help me in some way."

"I don't know what a school mascot is, but I do like hawks…"

Sequoia stood and barked several times.

"The dog is ready to travel," Finn said.

Chapter 20

Witch Island

They made their way down the trail with no interruptions from crows or other unknown creatures. The sun was setting in the west, and yellows, golds, and reds filled the sky. Elm knew they were drawing close to the river. He could smell the scent of fish, and it brought back memories of him fishing with his dad at the river near Oak Valley. A tear came to his eye, but he wiped it away.

"The river is around the next curve," Elm said. "I can smell it."

Randy agreed.

When the river came into view, Elm was surprised by the size. He and Willow stood on the bank, looking across the water. It was so large they couldn't see an island or any land. Tiny bugs flew over the water and a splash sounded in the distance.

"Can you eat the fish from this river?" Elm asked Finn.

"What?" Finn asked. "I don't eat animals, only fruits and grass."

Elm laughed. "Of course, you don't eat animals."

"Do you think we'll be safe crossing the river in a small boat?" Willow asked.

"Why do you think it will be a small boat?" Elm said.

"I don't know," Willow replied. "How many people or creatures do you think cross this river to witch island?"

Elm chuckled. "Witch island. I like that. Probably not too many fools go there."

As they settled on a slope, the sound of hooves could be heard pounding the ground, then Berthold stepped out of the brush with ten other centaurs.

"We've come to join you in your fight against the witch," Berthold announced.

Elm stood up. "Thanks. I'm sure we'll need all the help we can get." He pointed toward the pooka. "Finn is also going with us."

Berthold nodded to Finn.

"If you don't mind, I suggest you wait until morning to cross the river," Berthold said. "You don't want to go into a battle at night in a strange land."

"I agree," Elm said.

"While you rest through the night, we'll take turns watching over everyone." Berthold pointed to his comrades.

"Do we need to worry about being attacked by any vicious animals?" Elm asked.

A Murder of Crows

"No, but you might want to build a fire for some heat. The nights get cool by the river."

Elm and his group built two campfires—one near their sleeping bags and the other close to the resting centaurs.

After they got the fires going, they settled in for the night. Elm lay in his sleeping bag and gazed at the night sky. Stars decorated the sky and a half-moon shed a little light on the ground. He fell asleep thinking of his dad.

Elm jerked awake. He'd had a bad dream about Sequoia and the crow that had almost killed him. He searched the area. Sequoia lay next to Willow. He saw the centaurs standing guard. Relieved, he yawned and fell back to sleep.

A whistle—or was it a fog horn?—sounded loud with *toot-toot* which woke everyone. Elm rubbed his eyes and stared at the water. Next to the shore was a large sailboat resembling a pirate's ship.

"Gather your belongings—it's time to board the ship," Berthold said.

A long gangplank reached from the side of the ship to the shore, making it easier to board, especially for the centaurs. Once on deck, a tall, thin-as-a-rail man wearing a patch over one eye met them. His mustache hung down below his chin. He smiled—or was it a grimace?—and revealed several missing and rotten teeth.

"Hold on to something—this can be a very bumpy ride," he said in a gruff voice. He moved to the middle mast and pushed a button. Instead of a sail rising, material like a parachute flew up from the two outer poles. Once it was as high as it could go, Elm heard gears grinding beneath the deck. Looking up, he saw a giant fan spinning on the middle pole. The ship lifted into the air. Shaking and rattling, the ship sailed slowly above the vast river. Several times, long tentacles shot up from the water but were unable to reach the ship. Flying high in the sky, the only thing in sight was water.

"This river is gigantic," Elm said. "What's the name of the river?"

Berthold laughed. "It's the Neverending River."

"How long will it take to get to the island?" Randy asked.

"About an hour." The captain grunted. "Are you in a hurry to die?"

"I don't plan on dying." Elm nodded at Willow. They stepped away from the captain and leaned against a chest sitting in the middle of the boat. Randy, Lucinda, and Finn joined them.

Finally, the ship descended. It came to rest in the water next to the shore. As they went down the gangplank, the captain called after them, "Good luck. You're going to need it."

Up a hill they trudged with Elm in the lead. Almost near the top, he stopped behind a group of bushes. The land flattened between where they hid and a building.

"I can't believe it," Elm said. "It's the library, except it's dilapidated." The porch leaned, and the wood was rotten.

"It looks like a straight shot from here," Randy said. "Cross through those trees and up on the porch."

A Murder of Crows

"Those aren't trees," Berthold said. "They're carnivorous plants. The tall ones are pitcher plants. The smaller ones are Venus fly traps, and the ones spread across the ground are sundew vines."

"I should have paid more attention in class," Randy said.

They watched in horror as a crow flew out of a hole in the roof and dove toward something on the ground. As the crow flew back up, a goat flailed in its talons. The bleating sounded like a woman screaming. The bird dropped the goat into the pitcher plant.

"Oh my gosh, that's horrible," Elm cried as he spun around and looked at Sequoia. "You have to stay here until it's safe."

Sequoia growled, then growled again. He opened his mouth and "grrr, grrr, grrr" came out.

Berthold threw up his hands and gave a deep belly laugh. Finn rolled over on his back, laughing.

"What's wrong with you two?" Elm asked. "This is no laughing matter."

"Too bad you don't speak dog." Berthold laughed.

Finn wiped tears from his eyes. "Sequoia said he didn't live over a hundred years just to sit on the sidelines and not be part of the action or protect his family."

Elm and Willow squatted down and put their arms around the dog's neck. "I love you, Sequoia," Elm said. "We need to figure out a plan before we go running across the field and turn into crow bait for the plants."

"I volunteer," Finn said.

A Murder of Crows

"You volunteer for what?" Randy asked.

"I'm a pooka. I can change into a mouse, scurry across the field, do reconnaissance, and report back before we all go forward."

"Not a good idea," Berthold said. "You'll get trapped in the sundew vines."

"What about if I change into a tiny hummingbird? I could get a great bird's eye view."

"Aren't you afraid the crows will attack you?" Elm said.

"I know, I know," Lucinda said excitedly. "What about a bumblebee? Like you did before."

"That might work," Randy said.

The centaurs gave a thumbs up. Finn glanced at Elm for his approval.

"I agree," Elm said.

Finn grunted. His body shrank before their eyes. Wings popped out of his tiny body, and he buzzed around their heads several times before flying away. They sat down and waited. And waited. When Finn returned—

"What took you so long?" Elm said.

"Really? I was a bumblebee. How fast do you think I can fly? Anyway, the news is bad. No matter which direction you choose it will be treacherous."

"I don't see another way," Elm said. "Willow and Lucinda, run to the house. Fly like the wind across the ground. Maneuver over and around the sundew vines. Run as you have never run before. Randy and I will be behind you." Elm looked at Sequoia. "You do whatever you do."

"Elm, you're not making a lot of sense," Willow said.

"Just listen—Berthold, you and your group will flank us on both sides. We'll meet at the front door of the building. Be careful, and good luck to all of us."

Elm came out from where the group was hiding. Dark gray clouds hung low above them providing cover from the crows. They ran. Elm's pulse sped up when his first encounter was with the sundew vines. Instead of going in a straight line, he zig-zagged across at a slower pace, tiptoeing and jumping over the plants to make sure the sticky substance didn't touch him.

Elm heard a scream and watched as a sundew wrapped itself around one of the centaurs. In less than a minute, the plant had drained the life from the half-man half-horse.

Randy threw back his shoulders, ready for battle. He pulled his Swiss army knife out of his pocket and opened it to expose the scissors. "Let me go first. I can clip some of the vines and make a path."

The clouds parted, and the crows circled above them, casting shadows on the ground. Another scream came from the other side. Elm stood up. A crow dove—straight down—grabbing and carrying a centaur to a Venus fly trap. The bird dropped it. The crushing sound along with the screams was unbearable. Elm rushed to Willow's side. She bent over, then threw up.

"Don't think about it—keep moving." Elm looked at Randy. "How's it going with the scissors?"

A Murder of Crows

"They're all gummed up. I'm using the wire cutters, but they're also getting gummed up. But we only have about three feet to go, and we'll be out of this mess."

Elm saw the edge where the sundew vines stopped and a small clearing separated the vines from the Venus fly traps. They would be able stop for a few seconds to catch their breath.

As they stepped into the clearing, Elm lowered his voice. "Now that we're out of the sundews, our best chance is to move quickly and try to avoid the crows."

"That's easier said than done," Willow said. "But we're not that far from the building. We'll meet you on the porch." Willow and Lucinda charged across the yard.

The centaurs lined up in a single file. All of them held their crossbows at the ready. They would provide support for Elm and his group. The siege was on, and they rushed forward.

Elm, filled with exhaustion, ran as fast as he could with the others. Their lives depended on it. Crows circled above them. Arrows skimmed across the sky, striking birds here and there. The birds fell into sundew plants and Venus fly traps. The birds' sharp cries pierced Elm's ears.

Randy shrieked. A crow had him by his backpack and was taking him into the air. The crow dropped him into a pitcher plant. Sequoia raced to the plant. The dog chewed at the fibrous body where the flesh-digesting fluids resided.

Randy's voice could be heard above the noise of the crows. "I'm sliding. Help! I can't get out."

Willow and Lucinda placed their hands over their ears.

Only a few feet from the porch another crow charged toward Elm grabbing hold of his backpack. A smaller crow soared toward a bumblebee.

Finn flew straight for the Venus fly trap. The bird followed. When only an inch from Finn, the bird's wings touched the fly trap hairs, the plant slammed shut and crushed the bird. Finn, still a tiny bumblebee, escaped through the guard hairs of the plant.

Elm was dropped into a pitcher plant. He lay stuck to the sides of the plant near the top edge. In the distance, he heard Randy calling for help.

Elm took his cap off, which allowed him to lift his head. He could see over the side. Willow and Lucinda had made it to the porch of the house. Slowly, he slipped farther into the pitcher plant. Elm knew he had failed. His heart slowed down as he gave way to his fate. He spoke out loud, "Dad, I'm sorry I couldn't save you or my friends." He knew something like this would happen—the old oak tree had warned him if he came to this land, he would never leave. He now waited for his death.

A shadow passed over him. He blinked, unable to believe his eyes. The bird flew over him again—a white hawk.

The hawk hovered above Elm's head. Elm tried to lift his arms, but they were stuck to the plant. He heard the words, "Unbutton your shirt."

"What?" Elm said. "The hawk is talking? I'm dreaming, or I'm already dead."

A Murder of Crows

Again, the words came out of the hawk. "Unbutton your shirt."

"Finn, is that you?" Elm opened the front on his shirt.

The hawk lowered enough for Elm to grab hold of its legs. Struggling against the sticky goo, Elm was finally free from the plant, and the hawk carried him to the porch and set him down.

Finn turned back into a boy. "You told me you thought one day you would be saved by a white hawk. I thought I'd make that happen."

Elm hugged Finn. "Thanks for saving me." He turned around and saw everyone was on the porch. He cried out, "Randy! How? Oh my gosh, you stink."

"Sequoia chewed a large hole in the bottom of the plant," Randy said. "All of the digestive liquid drained out of the plant. When I slid down, I just kept going and came out the bottom. Now I'm covered in this awful smelling crap."

Elm turned toward Berthold. "Thanks to all the centaurs, we made it this far."

"I'm sorry to say, I lost two of my soldiers," Berthold said. "Their families will be devastated."

A loud cackling came from inside the house.

Chapter 21

Ultimatum

The front door hung askew, missing several hinges. They entered the building. The inside looked the same as the library except it was in complete disarray. Spiderwebs decorated the chandelier and hung across the walls. The staircase had more steps missing than it had leading up to the second floor. The witch was not in the main room.

Randy tilted his head. "I think I hear your dad's voice."

"Where's it coming from?" Willow asked. "What's he saying? Does he sound like he's in pain?"

"It sounds like it's coming from the second floor. He's talking to a child, telling her she'll be home soon."

Click, click—even on the rotten wood, Ms. Crow's heels clicked against the floor. She stood before them as a beautiful lady with a wide smile and not the old hag. "Too bad your dad is lying to the child. He's my next pick to feed to my plants. But I'm open to a deal."

Elm's jaw dropped. "What kind of deal?"

A Murder of Crows

He glanced at Willow. She looked concerned. He placed his hand on her shoulder.

Ms. Crow's expression looked arrogant and satisfied. "This was all for you, Elm. If you join me, I'll let everyone go home."

"No! I don't trust you. And why would you want me?"

Ms. Crow's smile widened. "You're not aware, but you and your sister are full of magic. I can teach you how to use it and become a great wizard. But you have to stay in this world."

Elm turned his back to Ms. Crow. All the centaurs stood around with their crossbows ready to fire and lariats by their sides. With knots in his stomach, Elm looked at Willow and Randy. "Maybe I should stay if it will save everyone."

"No," Willow said firmly.

Finn moved next to Elm and whispered something in his ear. Elm glanced at Berthold. He nodded his head.

"Enough talk," Ms. Crow growled. "what's your decision?"

Elm turned back to Ms. Crow. He took Willow's hand in his. Slowly raising their hands together, he pointed at the witch, and fire shot across the room. He waved their hands in a circle, and the fire surrounded Ms. Crow.

"Pooka, I'm going to kill you," Ms. Crow screamed. Her eyes were wide with fury.

"You're not going to kill anyone again," Elm yelled. "You are done."

Elm lowered their hands, and the fire dropped. The centaurs entered the circle and wrapped a magical rope around Ms. Crow. It would keep her from using her powers.

As the centaurs walked away with Ms. Crow encircled in their ropes, Berthold said, "Thanks, to you and your friends, Elm, our world will be safe again." He followed his group out the door.

"What are they going to do with her?" Willow asked Finn.

"You don't want to know," he replied. He handed Elm a bag. "This is fairy dust. If you sprinkle it over everyone, they won't remember anything that's happened to them."

"Thank you for everything you did, especially saving my life," Elm said.

Finn laughed. "It was an adventure. Thank you for letting me be a part of it. I have to go—the centaurs are waiting on me. You know what you have to do now."

"What did he mean, you know what to do?" Randy asked.

Before Elm could answer, a scream came from outside. They grew silent, the next sound they heard was the Venus fly trap's leaves slapping together, then the sound of bones crushing.

Elm looked at the door and said, "Goodbye, Ms. Crow." He faced Randy. "You, Lucinda, and Sequoia, find everyone and take them to the third floor. There should be a mirror that will take us back home. Don't go through it yet. Willow and I have something to do outside, then we'll meet you upstairs."

A Murder of Crows

Elm and Willow walked out of the building. The centaurs were leaving the area. A large white hawk flew over their heads and followed them.

"How did you know we had fire?" Willow asked. "What are we doing?"

"Finn told me when he whispered in my ear. Now we're going to burn down all these plants. Then we'll set the building on fire."

Together they raised their hands. Fire licked at the edges of the field, then spread quickly across all the plants. They went back into the building and started several small fires on the first and second floors. They hurried up the steps to the third floor where Randy, their dad, and the other kidnapped people waited for them in the tower room with the mirror.

"Randy, step out here for a minute," Elm said.

"What about me?" Lucinda asked.

"Sorry." Elm replied as he threw the fairy dust in the air and shut the door. "Count to ten."

Together they counted as smoke filled the air, making it hard to breathe. Elm kept his eye on the steps where crept upward like a hungry animal.

"Let's go," Elm said. "Willow, you go through the mirror first and as everyone comes through, get them out of the secret room and into the library."

Willow entered the room, laughing. "Okay, everyone, we're going to play a game. Take someone's hand and follow me."

Randy and Elm were last to step through the mirror. "Do you still have a hammer in your backpack?" Elm asked.

"Yes," Randy replied.

"Break the mirror into tiny pieces."

When Randy had completely obliterated the glass of the mirror, Elm closed the two sides of the mirror and tied a rope around it so it could never be opened again. They stepped out of the secret room.

Everyone milled around. Finally, Mr. Hardy said, "I'm glad everyone was able to participate in the scavenger hunt. I want to think Mr. Underwood for helping with this activity."

Everyone clapped and agreed they had a good time.

As they started down the steps to the lobby of the library, Kyle walked over with his arm around Lucinda. "I'm not sure what happened this weekend, but I'm glad you were there. This doesn't mean we're friends, flower boy."

"You're welcome," Elm said.

"And you—Wolff, well, you're just weird." Kyle and Lucinda walked away.

Elm laughed. "That's funny."

"What's funny?" Randy asked.

"Weird…weird Wolff. That's funny because it almost sounds like werewolf."

"Not funny, but maybe next month I'll dress up like one for Halloween." Randy snickered.

"I hope nothing strange happens next month," Elm said. "We have our birthdays to celebrate and then trick or treating. Can't wait for all that candy."

"You know Halloween was originally called All Hollow's Eve," Willow said. "It's when the spirits can rise up."

"If all we have to deal with is a couple of ghosts for a few hours, I think we can handle that," Elm said.

"Now that Ms. Crow is gone and hopefully everything is back to normal," Willow said, "I don't think we should go into the library or the cemetery next month. We'll just enjoy birthdays and Halloween."

"I agree," Randy said.

"Let's shake on it." Elm, Willow, and Randy piled their hands on top of each other and shook—but in the back of Elm's mind, he was planning a scavenger hunt in the cemetery.

Terry Nolan

Book Three

Coming in October 2022

About the Author

Her first novel, Forbidden Forest, was published in 2020. She was inspired one day while walking her dog, Ginger, through Hafer Park. She saw several children playing under large trees and they were surrounded by roots above the ground.

Now to continue the story of Elm Underwood, she has published A Murder of Crows.

She is originally from Delaware, now retired and living in Oklahoma with her dog, Ginger.